"Where you goin' with that stock, mister?"

Pat called as he rode into the path of the lead rider.

"Stevens, ain't it?" The man's watchful grin was flat. "All I can say is I'm under orders. This stuff must've been bought off yore spread while you was away."

The words came quick and curt. Clearly the man was bracing himself for anything that might come.

"Well, you won't be goin' any farther, anyway," Pat said, "till I've looked into it. First I want to see a bill of sale."

Seeing himself cornered, the man got tough. "You won't see nothin' but dust, hombre," he rasped. "Out of our way—"

Other Exciting Avon Westerns by
Peter Field

GUNS ROARING WEST

Coming Soon

RIDE FOR TRINIDAD!

A POWDER VALLEY WESTERN

DIG THE SPURS DEEP

PETER FIELD

AVON
PUBLISHERS OF BARD, CAMELOT, DISCUS AND FLARE BOOKS

AVON BOOKS
A division of
The Hearst Corporation
105 Madison Avenue
New York, New York 10016

Copyright © 1953 by Jefferson House, Inc.; copyright renewed in 1981
by Peter Field (pseudonym for L. W. Emerson)
Published by arrangement with Thayer Hobson & Company
Library of Congress Catalog Card Number: 87-91624
ISBN: 0-380-70421-8

First Avon Books Printing: January 1988

AVON TRADEMARK REG. U.S. PAT. OFF. AND IN OTHER COUNTRIES, MARCA
REGISTRADA, HECHO EN U.S.A.

Printed in the U.S.A.

K-R 10 9 8 7 6 5 4 3 2 1

1.

IT WAS CROWDING MIDNIGHT when the thin blade of a chill
September moon peeped out through a scatter of black clouds
to reveal a trim roan saddle-horse wearily threading the brush
not far from the Lazy Mare ranch headquarters, in southern
Colorado. Reaching the open ranch yard at last, the bronc
quickened its pace and with the instinct of a homing bird
made straight for the corrals.

In silence Pat Stevens slid lithely to the ground, stripped
off the sweat-stained hull and lifted it to a peg in the adjacent
saddle shed. Swinging the gate, then, he slapped the drooping
horse on the flank and watched it shamble into the corral,
where water and feed waited.

As he turned toward the house, Stevens's broad straight
back and easy stride betrayed nothing of his own tiredness,
after a grueling day in the hills. Habitual, keen-eyed alertness, even at this late hour, stamped him as still a young
man, hard, efficient, unemotional.

There was nothing about the silent ranch yard or its sleep-
ing buildings, familiar to Pat as his pockets, to arouse suspicion. Usually, when he was away till a late hour, it was true,
Crusty Hodge, his aging, grouchy handyman, left a lantern
burning in the kitchen, its wick turned low. Either Crusty had
forgotten it tonight, or the oil had burned out. Stevens made
no unnecessary noise as he mounted the steps and crossed the
narrow board porch to the door.

Despite his precautions, he expected nothing unusual tonight. A grunt of surprise wrenched out of him as, stepping
into the pitch-dark kitchen, he felt abruptly the rough grab of

1

a running noose, descending unseen over his head and pinning his arms to his sides as effectually as a vise.

"Hold it, hombre—right where yuh stand!" rasped a gruff voice.

Hauled forward a step by the sharp tug of the rope, Pat was unable instantly to pin down the vague familiarity he sensed in the words. As he braced himself taut, his quick ear caught the scrape of a match. A moment later the lamp on the table bloomed into light.

Pat found himself staring into the scowling round face of his squat and bow-legged friend, Sam Sloan. Six-gun in one hand, the rope firmly anchored in the other, Sloan stared for a brief space with no break in his stern severity, as if unable to credit his eyes. Then he relaxed.

"Oh. You, eh?" he growled. "Where in time yuh been keepin' yoreself till this ungodly hour, Stevens?"

Disgustedly, Pat twitched the rope free and flipped it off. He ignored the question, his own voice grating. "You might favor me with an explanation of why you're hangin' around my house—all primed and cocked with this kind of a reception!"

Despite his notable lack of warmth, Sloan grinned back at him, snaggle teeth showing in the rotund, cheerful face.

"That's easy." He nodded, his cool effrontery superb. "I'll just remind yuh of what happened to me once before, while I was waitin' here on the Lazy Mare for yuh at night. Shot at, an' chased plumb t' New Mexico by the Sheriff! I jest ain't takin' no more chances, for you or nobody!"

Pat's chuckle was a brief, explosive snort. "I'll concede that one—just so it don't happen again," he drawled. He paused then. "Was there somethin' you wanted?"

It was Sloan's turn to show annoyance. "Dang it, there yuh go!" he exclaimed. "Was there somethin' I wanted! . . . I'm blamed if I know why I bother to show any interest in an ornery crab like you, Stevens! Hereafter, if yuh want me to stay away altogether, I will!"

He seemed in deadly earnest. But knowing his chunky friend to the core, Pat only shrugged. "Come or go as you like," he grunted unfeelingly. "You do anyway—"

Sam's showy indignation was not proof against this kind of shrewd raillery. His grin flashed out again. "Yuh pegged me that time, boy . . . But where in tunket *have* yuh been all this while, Pat—if it ain't a closely guarded secret?''

Pat's headshake was minute. "It's no damned secret. Six or eight head of Lazy Mare stock disappeared again, Sam. That's the third time this month. I tried trackin' 'em—started this morning at daybreak—but it's the same old story once more. No luck.''

He shoved the coffee pot forward, chunked the stove as he spoke, and set out a brace of heavy china cups. Seating themselves, they looked at each other gravely over the lamp.

"Yuh lost their sign, huh?''

Pat brushed aside an imaginary gnat, with evident irritation. "Not for lack of trying," he said grimly. "Whoever's been workin' on my herd is a mighty smooth article!''

Sloan nodded thoughtfully. "Don't know who it could be, neither,'' he murmured. "Yuh ain't spotted nobody prowlin' around the spread, have yuh?''

Stevens's even white teeth showed briefly in his clean-cut bronze face. "Nobody but you—''

Ignoring the other's levity, Sam rasped his blue-stubbed jaw noisily in the heavy quiet. "There ain't been a stranger come into Powder Valley since what's-his-name—young Morgan—moved onto the Star Cross place, there in the hills.'' His glance lifted sharply to Pat's face. "Yuh don't reckon it could be *him*, do yuh?''

Pat delayed his answer. It was not his nature to do any wild guessing at such a time. Moreover, what little he knew of Ray Morgan, the blue-eyed redhead who had leased the little Star Cross a few months ago and had since striven single-handed to build up a paying spread, seemed largely to be all in that energetic young fellow's favor—precisely the impression aimed at by any man with crooked intentions, of course.

Frowning over his thoughts, Pat shook his head. "I don't know what to say, yet,'' he muttered. "Haven't been able to boil the signs down till they point unmistakably to any one man.''

"Ever talk to Morgan?'' Sam persisted.

Stevens nodded. "We've said howdy. He struck me as bein' pretty keen. Whether he's clever enough for this kind of work is another story.''

Sipping their coffee, they talked it over at length. Part

owner of a thriving horse ranch down the valley, and full time mentor and guardian of Pat Stevens—in his own eyes at any rate—Sloan showed a lively concern for his younger friend's fortunes, although at any time during the past few years Pat could have bought out him and his partner twice over.

"Dang queer yuh ain't able to trace them steers beyond yore own range," Sam declared. "Not once, but three times in a row!" Skepticism edged his voice.

Pat made another impatient gesture. "Every time they've been drifted over toward that malpais area below China Springs," he explained. "You know what that is. Even horseshoes won't leave a scratch there . . . I've spent my time tryin' to discover where they come out of it."

"China Springs, eh?" Sloan's glance was shrewd. "That ain't too far away from Morgan's Star Cross. Ever think of that?"

Pat spread his hands. "I've thought of it, sure. But it's facts I'm after, Sam."

They gave it up at a late hour, with Sloan still arguing warmly for energetic action—no matter what. At Pat's suggestion, because of the hour's lateness, Sam rolled into an extra bunk and stayed for the night.

They awoke early to the sound of Crusty Hodge banging the breakfast utensils about on the stove. A grumpy, taciturn piñon-knot of a man, unquestionably faithful to his keep, Hodge had not lain in his blankets after five in the morning or done a good hour's work during the day, in years. Pat tolerated his foibles out of the largeness of his nature, and Crusty silently repaid him with a grudging respect which he accorded to no other man on earth.

"Why can't yuh sleep till a decent hour?" growled Sloan, ruffling his tousled hair and knuckling his eyes as he entered the lamplit kitchen.

"We git up in th' mornin' here. If you don't like it," Crusty snarled at him, "gwan home an' stay there!"

Pat laughed heartily, standing in the kitchen door behind Sam. "That ought to hold you till breakfast," he told the latter.

Sam stumbled outside, muttering something that sounded

like "danged old fossil," and they heard him snorting and blowing as he washed up at the basin outside the door. A moment later his voice rose afresh in truculent argument. Pat glided to the opening for a quick look.

A lanky, broad-shouldered man sat his bronc in the yard. Gaunt of features, his auburn hair grizzled, he had lost none of the fierce energy of inveterate youth. He glared out of his single eye as if Sam were his worst enemy.

"Don't gimme no song an' dance," he roared, piercing the little man with a look of blistering accusation. "Why didn't yuh come home last night, where yuh belong?"

It was Ezra, Sloan's partner in the little Bar ES horse spread, and by no means a bad man to have at one's back.

"Go jump in the wash, yuh old crow," Sam bawled, with cheerful energy. "Never occurred to yuh I'd mebby enjoy a night away from yore naggin' tongue, huh? Wal, I did—an' here I am!"

"Get down, Ezra, and come in," Pat broke through their bickering with scant ceremony. "You're just in time for breakfast. Maybe a bite or two'll sweeten Sam's disposition."

"I'll need *some* help t' wring sense out of 'im," Ezra muttered, sliding out of the saddle and striding forward.

Sitting down shortly to a generous meal, the big man listened with interest to Pat's description of the rustling. If he showed no surprise it was because he had learned to look for the unexpected during the devious course of a rough-and-tumble existence.

"The China Springs malpais, yuh say?"

He pondered the meager facts soberly. "We'll ride out there this mornin' for a look around. Seems like somethin' kin be done."

His matter-of-fact assumption that little, if anything at all, had as yet been done, would have been ludicrous but for the fact that, despite the handicap of his eyesight, Ezra was by far the best tracker they had ever known, and certainly the peer of any in this section of the West.

"It'll be appreciated," Pat assured him simply. "I've done all I'm able to, and I'm up against a blank wall."

Accordingly, the trio pulled away from the Lazy Mare on fresh broncs just as the sun broke over the eastern hills, dispelling the crisp chill of the early fall night. An hour's jog brought them to China Springs, on the western fringe of Stevens's extensive holdings, and here Ezra motioned the others back while he had a deliberate look around.

"What yuh make of it, Ez?" called Sam after a delay.

The lanky man's answer took the form of a counter query. "Yuh been grazin' stuff in here recent, Stevens?" he demanded.

Pat shook his head. "Just happens I haven't needed the grass this season," he replied. "Why?"

"Eight or ten head been watered here lately," returned Ezra. "Some hombre was handlin' 'em. I see the marks of his bronc."

"Uh-huh. Wal, what we wanta know is where he went from here," interjected Sloan dryly.

Ezra slanted a brief glance in Sam's direction, but offered no rejoinder. He went on casting about, his maneuvers taking him gradually toward the south. In a short time he had worked a considerable distance away.

"Where yuh goin'? The spring's way over here," Sam barked at him testily.

"Want me t' track them steers, don't yuh?" Ezra snapped. "Wal, that's what I'm doing'—"

Following at a little distance, Sloan stared down at the rocky ground with amazed incredulity. "Yuh mean t' say you're readin' signs—here? *I* can't see a thing."

"Yuh can't?" Ezra's sarcasm was immense. "Mebby it's a good thing *I'm* doin' this, instead o' you."

It was plain to Pat as time passed that the one-eyed giant had caught a warm scent. The way led through a tangled maze of ragged lava, where it seemed impossible that any trail could be picked up. Often Ezra was admittedly at fault, but he patiently puzzled out the faint trail. Steadily he worked toward the southern border of the rugged malpais.

Seeing how matters went, Pat circled and drifted ahead, beginning to work back and forth through the mesquite beyond the rocks. Ten minutes later the partners heard his hail.

"Okay, Ez. We've brought 'em this far," Pat called.

Ezra and Sam hurried forward and joined him. The former's sharp scrutiny picked up the plain imprint of hoofs winding through the brush. He nodded. "Ought t' be a cinch from here out."

They followed the trail of the steers more rapidly now. From time to time as they advanced, Sam lifted his gaze for a shrewd scrutiny of their surroundings. It was not yet midday when Stevens heard the little man's soft snort of discovery.

"Thought so," Sam exclaimed triumphantly. "Notice where we're headin' now, don't yuh, Pat?"

"Yuh mean—?"

Sam's nod was grim. "Straight for young Morgan's Star Cross," he affirmed. "I began t' catch on half an hour ago. Now I'm sure!" He pointed significantly across the brushy swells where, almost directly ahead of them, a clump of cottonwoods marked the location of the little Star Cross ranch, its buildings grouped in a shallow cup of the hills.

Pat's lingering glance in that direction was speculative and thoughtful. "It certainly looks—" he began colorlessly, only to break off abruptly. "Stick with the trail, you two," he told the others, then. "I'll jog on ahead. There's a slim chance I may catch Ray Morgan at home."

Lifting his reins he cruised forward, making directly for Morgan's place. As he neared the cottonwoods, minutes later, he veered so as to keep cover between himself and the clapboard ranch house, meanwhile scrutinizing the yard with care. No signs of life met his eye. Still he moved forward circumspectly. Anyone working about the place—unless on the sharp lookout for just such a visit—would have been caught unawares of Pat single-footed into the yard from behind a shed.

But there was no one to notice his arrival. The place appeared singularly deserted, almost abandoned, without even a nondescript dog to raise a mild clamor.

Pat was still sitting his saddle, a doubtful look on his face, when he caught sight of Ezra and Sam working their way close. They did not advance directly, but forged on through the thin brush. Pat rode out to join them, and they met a few yards away from Morgan's pole corral.

"Stevens, here's where them steers went!" Ezra stabbed a gnarled finger bluntly at the corral. "Ain't no doubt about it!"

Pat shrugged. "If my Lazy Mare stuff landed here, it was only a way station," he observed. "There's still work to do, Ez."

They could not doubt what he meant, for the corral was empty. Ezra only turned away, proceeding to cast about the spot. A few minutes later he was off on a new tack, working steadily toward the hills. Without comment he led the way rapidly, scarcely seeming to study the ground as he followed the plain trail of the little bunch of steers.

The mesquite thinned as they climbed, giving place to scattered buffalo grass. Gradually the range grew richer. As Pat expected, the time came when the tracks they were following merged with those of other steers until the lanky tracker was forced to haul up, scratching his head in bafflement.

"End of the line, Ez?" asked Pat quietly.

The big fellow was stubborn. "Not much! No sense quittin' after comin' this far—"

"Seems to be any number of arroyos around here, where a handful of beeves could hide," Pat remarked. "We'll have our look around."

It was well they did so. Not twenty minutes later, Sam's rolling whoop brought the others on the run to where he sat his bronc atop a crumbling cut-bank. Pat gazed over and down. Below in the wash, heads nodding as they rested out the noonday warmth of the sun, were eight brindled steers, all two- and three-year-olds, fat and prosperous, and all wearing Pat's familiar Lazy Mare brand on their flanks.

"Wal! There's yore stock, Stevens!" Ezra exclaimed in a pleased tone. "Reckon that settles that."

For a space, however, Pat neglected to speak, his mind already probing far beyond this point. The fact that the steers were still grouped in a close bunch, so far away from their home range, was glaring proof that they had been rustled. But how far beyond that had they got?

Sam read his thought. "Soft-hearted Stevens," was his caustic jibe. "Even now yuh hate t' break down an' admit to yoreself that young Morgan's a crook!"

"I'd hate to come to any such conclusion about any man," Pat returned stubbornly. "Not that I'd hesitate a second, once I was dead sure—"

"What in creation more do yuh want?" challenged Sam hotly. "Tracked the stuff straight t' Morgan's doorstep, didn't we? It's still bein' hid out on his range! Dang it all—"

"Hold on, Sam." Stevens's tone was level. "You know

the law on rustlin'. 'Less you grab a man red-handed, brandin'
or drivin' stolen stock, you haven't proven guilt. This looks
bad, yes. But I'm still not sold on Ray Morgan's part in this
business.'' He lifted an admonishing hand as the crusty partners both attempted to speak at once. ''Not a word, now! I'll
play this hand my own way. You two'll play it the same, or
not at all . . . Sorry, but that's how it's got to be.''

2.

"Yuh lookin' around to see if yuh can locate Morgan?" Sam Sloan asked, a trace of huffiness in his tone.

Pat looked at him with exaggerated dignity. "First thing I intend to do, now I've laid hold of these steers, is to drive 'em back home where they belong."

"Sense t' that," Ezra grunted, a brief smile touching his weathered lips. "Let's git goin!"

No more was said as they headed the Lazy Mare stock toward Stevens's range and hustled it along. Pat kept a narrow watch about them, not unaware of threatened danger even now, should the frustrated rustler be lingering anywhere in the vicinity. But they were not molested. Early afternoon saw the recovered steers turned loose on their home ground.

"Thanks a heap, boys," Pat said to his friends as they turned away. "Headin' for Dutch Springs and home, I expect? I'll ride in to town with yuh, and we'll damp the dust down."

They rode into the little one-street cowtown an hour later, three abreast, their usual good-humored comradeship restored once more. Friends hailed them as they passed down the street. If his companions remained unimpressed by all this attention following a recent adventure, Sloan made up for their reserve. He waved and sang out jovially a dozen times, exhibiting his genial, moonfaced grin.

They were dismounting before the Gold Eagle when Sam paused, one foot still in the stirrup, to gaze fixedly up the street.

"Stevens," he muttered, never shifting his glance for a second. "Take a look!"

Turning smoothly, his look following the other's, Pat was not greatly surprised to observe the object of their recent attentions, Ray Morgan, a couple of hundred yards farther along the boardwalk, before Jeb Winters's general store.

Just now Morgan was talking to a girl in trim riding clothes and divided skirt, her straw-colored hair curling out from under a cocky Stetson. So preoccupied was he that he seemed oblivious of anything else about him.

"Who is that he's buzzin'?" growled Ezra, squinting out of his one eye. "Old Zep Cowan's girl, ain't it?"

"It's Candace Cowan." Pat nodded musingly. "Morgan's a fast worker, I'll say that much for him. She's one of the nicest girls in the valley—"

"You got it too, eh?" Sloan grunted approvingly. "Looks like she's almost beggin' Morgan to do somethin' or other. Is he playin' hard t' get?"

They watched a moment or two longer. It was certainly true that the girl appeared to be pleading with young Morgan; and just as plainly he seemed reluctant to comply with her wishes, whatever they were.

'Yuh figurin' to step down there?" Ezra queried.

Strangely enough, Pat had not yet made up his mind, and his glance lingered on the young couple speculatively. Thus it happened that he was looking that way when Morgan whirled without warning to swing heavily at a man who had paused an arm's length away, and knock him down.

Ezra and Sam saw it, too. In unison the three mens started that way impulsively, striding along the boardwalk.

The man felled by Morgan sprang to his feet with a bellow. Gnarled, raw-boned and heavy-set, perhaps twenty years the other's senior, he appeared a formidable antagonist, whipping over a right cross which sent the redhead heeling around.

"Hey!" Sam exclaimed, staring. "That's Pike Tigart Morgan's pitched into—"

"Right the first time," said Ezra grimly. "An' a grizzled old wolf he is, too!"

Pat was so far from disagreement with these findings that he drew to a halt to watch narrowly, his strong lips folded into a straight and narrow line. "Hold on," he told the partners in an undertone. "Let's just see how this comes out."

Others were ahead of them. A dozen men surrounded the combatants in a loose circle, and more came hurrying forward. Pat noted that Candace Cowan held her place in the ring, her piquant oval face pale, but without any other sign of distress.

Her gaze was riveted on Morgan's faintly freckled face, just now a frozen mask of wrath and determination. Lean almost to lankiness, young Ray was too shrewd to close with his huskier antagonist. Hovering at arm's length even while he carried the fight, he systematically slashed at Tigart's hard, bony cheeks and outthrust jaw. It was bitter punishment, but Pike showed no inclination to retreat. Ramrod of the huge Flagg ranch, north of the valley, he was a hard-bitten character. Veteran of a hundred such affairs in his time, certainly he intended to emerge from this one without any marked loss of prestige.

One of Ray's blows hurt him. With a roar, he rushed at Morgan, striving to grapple with him. Blue eyes blazing, the redhead was cocked and ready. Driven backward on rocking heels, he slammed solidly against the ring of watchers, then, regaining his balance, unleashed a haymaker that bounced off Tigart's hatless scalp with a meaty smack.

Pike spun around. He staggered wildly, arms flung out, trying to get his legs under his weight. Morgan sprang forward, watching keenly for the perfect opening. Just as he set himself for a solid stance, every muscle coiled for the kill, a cowboy broke out of the circle and, whether by accident or design, thrust out a booted foot. Ray tripped over it, pitched forward, and nearly went flat.

A yell went up as half-a-dozen men laid rough hands on the puncher and hurled him back. Tigart took swift advantage of the situation, recovering and leaping toward his enemy. A chopping blow, and Morgan suddenly collapsed, knocked off his pins. Torn face set, the Flagg foreman closed on his victim. A boot lashed out, a sledge-hammer fist lifted.

Before it could descend, an aroused bellow broke the taut silence. A big, broad-shouldered man crowded close. Iron fingers clamped on Tigart's arm and wrenched him around.

"What's the story here?" rasped a voice as harsh as a file.

It was Jess Lawlor, the Dutch Springs sheriff. Tigart scowled up into his rugged face, thunderstruck. After a pause he jerked back angrily, striving to free himself.

"Leggo, Lawlor—!"

Jess relinquished his grip deliberately. "Stand hitched, mister," he rumbled in warning, "or I'll crack yore neck! What's the idea of beatin' up young Morgan here, anyhow?"

"Hell, he never!" exclaimed a ruffled voice from the sidelines. "Morgan had him plumb groggy two minutes ago—"

"Yeh! Till he was tripped—by one of Pike's own Flagg punchers," another man interposed scathingly.

Tigart brushed this attack aside stolidly. "No matter who done it! He had it comin'," he growled. "I near had Morgan then. An' I'd of finished him, too!"

Lawlor surveyed him with severe impartiality. "Yuh would, huh? Who started it?"

"Morgan did—damn him!" Tigart ripped out vindictively. "Jumped me without an I, yes or no, Lawlor, as I was comin' up-street! I ain't takin' no shovin' around—from him, or nobody else!"

If his rocky defiance included the Sheriff, as it seemed to do, the imperturbable lawman declined the challenge, rasping his chin in thoughtful silence. The gathered men moved, parting, as Ray Morgan got unsteadily to his feet. Lawlor turned to him heavily.

"What about this, feller?" he demanded. "Yuh heard Tigart's talk—"

Staring hard at Tigart, the uncowed redhead looked ready to jump the man afresh at a second's notice. "Sure, I climbed him."

"What for?"

"Ask him." Morgan's cool self-possession displayed no flaw.

Tigart snarled at the words, his features suffused with red. "That's no answer," he bawled. "Don't let 'im get away with this, Sheriff!"

"*He* knows why I turned on him—if he'll tell," Morgan repeated. "You're damned lucky I didn't sink a slug in yore rotten carcass, Tigart! You know that, too, smart guy!"

"That'll be enough of that talk," Lawlor growled, shooting glances from one to the other in some perplexity. "Somethin' queer here, that's plain. But I won't stand for no rough stuff here in town, Morgan. Get it through yore head, because next time I won't stop with a warnin'!"

"You can go ahead right now," the young fellow tossed back flatly. "Do what yuh want, Lawlor, if it'll make yuh feel any better!"

Jess's face tightened at this brazen invitation. Its sole effect was to make him study Morgan more closely.

"Mean anything special by that?" he ground out.

"I should smile I do!" Ray's retort was a drawl. "Inquire into what's behind all this, Sheriff—as you'll have to, if yuh carry this any further—and you'll be doin' *me* a favor—not Tigart. Or have yuh already suspected as much?"

"Chase the danged young nuisance out of town, Lawlor," exclaimed the Flagg foreman, with betraying haste.

Lawlor scanned them both with faint disfavor. Whether the pair were range rivals was a matter of comparative indifference to him, used as he was to the endless feuding of cattlemen. Concerning his own stand he chose to leave no uncertainty whatever.

"If there's somethin' between yuh, leave it where it started," he ruled. "I won't tolerate no rows in the street. Start another one, Morgan, an' I'll see that yuh have time to think it over in private!"

It was his last word, and he turned to shove away. The watchers, following his example, slowly drifted off. Hard-faced, young Morgan stood his ground, not moving out of his tracks; and it was Tigart who turned to lead his offending puncher away, ignoring the covert looks cast in their direction.

Candace Cowan had disengaged herself from the affair on Sheriff Lawlor's arrival and moved unobtrusively away. Pat saw Morgan glance about in search of her, without result.

"Now's yore chance at that hombre, Stevens, if yuh don't intend to speak t' Lawlor about him," Sam Sloan murmured, nudging the other. "Aim t' jump Ray about those cows, or don't yuh?"

Watching young Morgan soberly from a distance of a dozen yards, Pat shook his head slowly and decidedly. "Not now, Sam," he replied quietly.

"Not now, he says! Wal." The little bantam snorted sarcastically. "Might's well forget it for good, then!" A note of curiosity stole into his voice. "What would be holdin' yuh back, for cramp sake?"

Stevens calmly ignored the sarcasm. "It suits me to watch what goes on here, without interference—"

"Yuh mean yuh think it ain't over?" Sloan's bushy brows arched. "Dang it, yuh heard Lawlor warn young Morgan t' lay off—!"

Pat's thin smile was tolerant. "Who said it was Morgan that was pushin' this thing?" he retorted. "I never suggested anythin' of the kind, because I don't believe it's true . . . Although I judge that boy to be pretty well able to take care of himself in a fight."

It was more than Sam could swallow. "That's right—worry about him, now! First thing we know, yuh'll be leadin' Morgan by the hand. Only don't expect *us* t' help bring back yore next bunch o' rustled steers!" He turned to his lanky partner. "Let's go, Ez. I know my own mind, at any rate. If *he* wants us for anythin', which I doubt, he knows where he can find us!"

It suited Pat's book to let them move off in a pretended dudgeon. Much as he liked the pair—and much as he owed them—there were times when he could do without their company, and this happened to be one of them.

If he had hoped that Ray Morgan, seeing him alone, might make any advances on his own account, however, he was to be disappointed. With Candace gone from view, Morgan turned away, going about his own affairs. Pat contented himself with keeping the other in sight at a distance, it being no part of his intention to call himself deliberately to the young fellow's attention.

Morgan's chores appeared wholly commonplace as he moved around town, taking no pains to avoid running into Tigart, the Flagg foreman, nor on the other hand seeming in the slightest to court this. If he was looking for Candace Cowan, that fact did not make itself obvious, either.

Pat exercised this lazy surveillance, and thought his own thoughts, at last glancing toward the declining sun. The afternoon was fast waning. Sam and Ezra, comfortably established in the Gold Eagle, he had not seen for some time. Should he delay his return home to the Lazy Mare until he had watched young Morgan leave town? It seemed hardly worth while to make it an issue, one way or the other.

Stepping into Jeb Winters's store for a sack of smoking, he all but collided with a girl in the act of emerging. His hat came off in haste.

"Howdy, Candace." He paid her the compliment of close, admiring attention. "Sorry if I bumped yuh—"

She gave him a saucy, laughing glance. "You men! I don't think for a minute it was accidental." Her roguish look turned backward as she swept on out. "But you're forgiven this time, Mr. Stevens!"

Pat was still smiling to himself as he paid for his tobacco. Returning to the store porch, and glancing up and down the street, he noted that the girl had already disappeared. Evening was closing in, the long shadows deepening.

Next moment he noticed Ray Morgan making hurriedly for the high-fenced public corral beyond the jail. On his way home, doubtless. The Star Cross man passed through the wooden-arched gate to disappear from sight. Five minutes later he had not reappeared. Pat grunted.

"Funny. What could be holdin' him up?"

Stevens stepped off the store porch and sauntered that way without haste. Still Morgan failed to put in an appearance. It was far from Pat's design to follow him into the corral, however. Reaching the place, he paused, propping a shoulder lightly against the weathered board fence. Not by accident had he selected a spot beside a large crack.

As he expected, voices could be heard inside, speaking quickly, now low, now urgent. Pat suddenly understood where Candace Cowan had so quickly disappeared to. She was in the corral, alone with Morgan. And once more she was pleading with the young fellow, as she had done earlier in the street. Pat's ears pricked up at the tenor of her words.

"Please, Ray." There could be no mistaking her important tone. "I ask you to get away from Dutch Springs before dark. You keep asking why—but it seems little enough!"

"Sure. An' I'm considerin' who asks it," came Morgan's mutter. "But, Candy, I've had a plenty! *He* ain't shovin' me around. Hell with him! I'll leave town when I get ready—"

The girl's voice broke in so quickly as to make the words unintelligible. But from the strength of her plea, Pat drew his own surprised conclusions regarding the true measure of her attachment to this young man. His safety was a matter of vital concern to her, and just as certainly she considered it to be gravely endangered.

Pat would have unblushingly listened longer. But just then, glancing absently down-street, he observed a man coming that way, purpose in his brisk stride. With a jar, Pat recognized Pike Tigart. The Flagg foreman must have watched Morgan, for he was making straight for the corral.

Pat had never had more than casual dealings with the man and did not particularly like him. Nor did he wish to call the other's notice to himself now. Shoving away from the fence, he stepped to the corral gate, slipped quietly inside, turned at once toward a rig hitched in the near corner, and moved behind it.

As he expected, Morgan and the girl were so ingrossed in their own affairs as to overlook his arrival entirely. Their voices lowered slightly, but went on. Pat heard Tigart's boots scuff at the entrance and pause there. Pat sneaked a look across the backs of the horses. It was gloomy inside this high enclosure, but not yet dark.

Pike saw Morgan. His harsh face hardened. He started forward.

"Wal, Morgan!" Tigart's voice grated like sand. "Ain't pullin' out without a little talk, I hope?"

Candace whirled and froze, staring at him. Ray moved apart from her without speaking. His whip-hard frame went taut, his bitter gaze fastened on the Flagg foreman.

"No talk," he ripped out. "We'll settle it here an' now, Tigart!"

It was obvious to Stevens that Pike Tigart should have taken warning from this. He appeared not to do so, continuing his deceptively indolent advance. "Oh, no doubt yore friend'll help us reach an agreement," he drawled, only his beady, pitiless eyes betraying his real purpose. He was within a dozen feet of the two, when Morgan abruptly leveled a condemning finger.

"Stop right there, Tigart!" he said thinly. "Not another step—!"

Pike paused tentatively, in exaggerated surprise. "Yuh don't trust me, boy?" His laugh was a croak. "What'll yuh do—*hey?*"

The last word cracked like a whip, as he took another step forward. If he meant to crack Morgan's nerve, however, he failed signally of his purpose. Without the slightest hesitation or change of expression, Ray went for his gun.

Whether Tigart expected the move or not, he believed himself prepared for it. His own hand blurred, flashing to his hip. Morgan's Colt roared flatly before Pike got the gun levelled. The weapon dropped from his grasp to bounce away. Tigart staggered back, grabbing his torn hand with the other.

"Yuh shot me!" he bawled. "Damn yuh, this is yore finish, punk!"

Morgan's gunbarrel unconsciously lowered. He and Candace stared at the man. Before they could gather their wits, Pat Stevens burst out on them, running forward.

"Yuh heard him, Morgan! It'll be true, if you're grabbed here now! Get that gun out of sight, and pull out of here fast!" he ordered curtly.

Not yet fully comprehending what was taking place, Morgan shot a dismayed look at the girl. He hesitated.

"Never mind Candace!" Pat rifled at him. "I'll look after her. Stir your stumps, man! Make yourself scarce!"

"Ray—go. Do as he says!" Candace exclaimed. "You must know you can never face this out and win, after this afternoon!"

Suddenly alive to the situation, Morgan whirled. Raised voices could be heard down the street. In a matter of fleeting seconds men would dome running. Escape would be cut off.

Ray sprang to his horse, whipped the reins free, and rose swiftly to the saddle. The bronc reared and came down hard, then tore for the gateway. An instant, and horse and rider flashed through and were gone. A diminishing tattoo of flying hoofs drifted back to them, fast fading to silence.

3.

THE FIRST PERSON to come running into the corral was Sheriff
Lawlor. The light was rapidly fading here; he peered hard at
the trio he found waiting, and slowed abruptly. The bony
fingers curling round the handle of his run relaxed as he
caught sight of Pat. His sharp glance ran to Tigart, standing
there nursing his injured hand and cursing.

"Wal. What now?" the lawman demanded grimly.

"Dammit, Jess—skip the details!" Pat was unusually curt.
"Yuh can see this man's in tough shape. Better get him to the
doctor in short order—"

It was true enough. Tigart's leathery face was pasty and he
was none too steady on his feet, the blood dripping from his
torn hand in a steady trickle. He stared at Pat, then turned to
Lawlor with a lurch.

"Yuh ain't takin' me nowheres!" he got out thickly. "I
got plenty t' say—!"

Other men had arrived, hurrying into the corral and gathering about. "All right, boys. Some of yuh get him to Doc
Barker right off." The Sheriff paid scant attention to Tigart's
gruff protests. "Take it easy, Pike," he called after him as he
was led away. "Neither of us is leavin' town. I'll see yuh,
don't fret."

He turned back to face Pat, with an unconscious alternation
of his rather ponderous manner. "I must say I'm a little
surprised at yuh, Stevens," he said heavily. "Mind tellin' me
what set that fracas off?"

Pat's shrug was indolent. "The surprise is mutual, Jess,"
he said with artless frankness, flashing his engaging grin.
"But Tigart deliberately picked a quarrel, and one thing led

19

to another." He made an expressive gesture. "What could a man do—?"

Lawlor cleared his throat, scrutinizing him closely. Standing beside them Candace started to speak, only to break off abruptly and stare at Pat in amazement. Lawlor ignored her.

"Swearin' there was no overt provocation, are yuh?"

Pat's innocent expression was perfect. "I didn't do a thing to him."

The lawman's comment was measured. "You're one of mighty few men I'd let get away with this, Stevens," he said. "It'll keep till I've talked with Tigart, anyhow."

Candace's hand came out in an impulsive gesture, stopping just short of Pat's arm. It had taken her a few seconds to grasp fully what was happening here; but she knew now that without any actual false statements, Pat Stevens was allowing the Sheriff to gather that it was he who had shot Tigart. Nor did it escape her that, by his instigation, the Flagg foreman had been hustled away before he had a chance to spill the beans. That Pat was deliberately covering for Ray Morgan she could not help seeing clearly. What his motive could be was less clear.

"Yes, Candace?" Lawlor had noticed her start. But Pat's smiling inquiry was serene.

"I— Nothing." The girl spoke hurriedly, smothering the words crowding on her tongue.

Jess had his own noncommittal glance at her face. If he was asking himself what was in her mind, he did not show it. After a few more words with Pat he turned away. Candace waited only until he had drawn beyond earshot, her manner uneasy, but before she could speak, another voice broke in on them edgily.

"Smart of yuh, Stevens. Mighty smart!"

Pat glanced indifferently toward Sam Sloan and Ezra, standing a few yards away. "First time you found that out?" he countered briefly.

Sloan's head nodded with knowing assurance. "Give us the lowdown," he proposed softly. "It was a smooth job of coverin' up. All we need t' know is what was behind it!"

Pat accepted this with dignified reserve. "Cover-up?" he echoed colorlessly, as if failing to understand. "What yuh talkin' about, Sam?"

"Yuh never shot Pike Tigart!" the little man said flatly. "You know it, an' I know it!"

"Pat, it *was* fine of you," Candace broke in unexpectedly. "But the truth must come out, of course, as soon as Jess Lawlor has his talk with—that man."

"Sure, it will—yuh dang dunce!" Sloan seconded.

Pat surveyed all three of them smilingly. "Sure of that, are you?"

It was Ezra who spoke up now, peering at Stevens hard. "Yuh may have somethin' there," he murmured. "Chances are Jess Lawlor knowed what was goin' on all the time—" Candace gasped as his meaning came home to her. "Then Ray is all the more obliged to you," she exclaimed. "But what led you to do such a thing, Pat?"

Pat waved a hand airly. "You're all makin' a fuss about nothing. Whatever it is yuh think I did, it seemed like the thing to do. Shall we let it go like that?"

Eza and Sam would have had a great deal more to say had not the girl's presence deterred them. They did not intend for her to carry their frank suspicions back to Morgan. She was not done yet, however.

"Surely Ray will want to thank you, once he knows this," she declared warmly. "You must give him that opportunity—"

"Don't worry." Pat spoke solidly. "I've been plannin' to have a talk with that young feller. He'll get his chance to speak his piece, if I have to go out of my way to give it to him."

"Wal, there's still Tigart t' be considered," said Sam gravely. "He won't like yuh, Stevens, when he learns yore game."

Pat smiled confidently. "I don't believe he'll make any fast moves for a while."

"No? . . . Mighty tough crew behind that hombre," Sam said shrewdly. "Don't forget that."

Pat's shrug said that he would overlook nothing. "I've taken my chances in the past. I expect I'll have to do the same this time."

He put Candace in her buckboard and saw her safely off for the Bull's Head, her father's ranch, a dozen miles east on the Hopewell Junction trail. With the crusty partners, he moved up to the Gold Eagle for a nightcap; and if the pair heckled him irritably about his suspicious actions, it all slid off his capable back. Ray Morgan of the Star Cross was one topic he flatly refused to discuss.

But if he would not air his opinions concerning Morgan, it was not because he had none. The younger man was much in his mind during the ride home to the Lazy Mare. Moreover, the following morning Pat was up early. In the gray dawn he saddled and headed directly for the little Star Cross spread with stern purpose in his manner.

The sun was an hour high and growing warm when he drew near Morgan's place. It was a fresh and sparkling day, the brush a ripe dun against the clear blue sky. Pat paid scant attention to this quiet beauty, scrutinizing with care the weathered clapboard ranch house under the cottonwoods and paying special heed to the sagging sheds.

He saw no movement as he approached. It was necessary to draw quite close to look down into the little hollow, and he was not more than a hundred yards away when a ripping sound slashed unwarningly through the brush-tops near at hand, followed by the rolling crack of a carbine.

Throwing his bronc sidewise, he raced toward a nearby wash. Even as he slid precipitately into this shelter, a second slug whined over his head, uncomfortably close.

"If that's Morgan, it's mighty plain he craves no company," he said to himself grimly, losing no time in getting to a safe distance from the concealed marksman at the ranch.

There was no pursuit, not did he expect any. That it was not his plan to leave without accomplishing his purpose, however, became plain when he began circling into the hills, sticking to Star Cross range, but giving the ranch buildings a wide berth. His mind was busy as he rode. He could readily understand Morgan's wanting no visitors after yesterday's events, but if it was indeed Ray himself who had fired those shots at him, it threw an entirely different light on the young fellow.

He was soberly canvassing this possibilty, driving on through intervals of scrub pine and parklike meadowland fringing the hills, when, breaking through a line of trees, he came abruptly on a scene far different from anything he had expected.

Seeking water, a yearling calf had got itself thoroughly bogged in a muck hole, and with a loose rope over its head,

Ray Morgan was busily doing his best, with the aid of his cowpony, to extricate the animal. Catching sight of Pat, Morgan froze watchfully, in obvious doubt as to what to expect. He waited for the other to speak.

"Howdy, Morgan," Pat halted at a respectable distance, ostensibly to note the predicament of the Star Cross calf.

Ray's acknowledgement of the salutation was scarcely effusive. "That you doin' the shootin', down at my ranch a while back?"

Pat looked at him directly now, showing faint surprise. "Me? No." His denial was a grunt.

"Who was it, then?" Morgan's words continued curt and suspicious.

Pat shrugged his shoulders. "I tell yuh it wasn't me," he insisted mildly. "What would I be bangin' away at down there?"

Morgan had his own brisk way about him, thought upon thought leaping in his wary mind. "What about it, Stevens? Did Candace get away all right last night?"

"Why not? I saw her off myself." Pat's smile was disarming. "Take it easy, will yuh, Morgan?"

Ray's alert glance rested watchfully on Pat's hands, refusing to lift to his face. His tone did not soften. "Why should I?"

Pat showed faint resignation. "I will say I rode over here expectin' to have a sensible talk with yuh. But if that's the way you look at things, we'll skip it."

At least he had Morgan's close attention now. The latter paused, his blue eyes slitted.

"I don't get yuh, Stevens. What would you have to talk to me about?"

The defiance was plain. Pat's manner grew offhand. "A matter of six or eight Lazy Mare steers that disappeared off my range a couple of days ago. They were tracked straight to your Star Cross corral, Morgan, and later we picked 'em up a mile or so off in the hills." His voice grew stern as he ended. "What can yuh tell me about it?"

Morgan stared at him for a long moment as if petrified, giving no heed to the bawling of the mired calf.

"Yores, were they?" he said finally, straightening in the saddle. Pat continued to watch him curiously, without answer. "I never rustled 'em, Stevens!" Ray concluded doggedly, biting the words off.

"That wasn't what I asked yuh—"

"I don't know a thing about it, I tell yuh," Morgan insisted, his face closed. "I didn't steal 'em, and you can make what yuh want of it!"

"Hell, I never thought you did, man!" Pat pretended strong impatience. "If I did, yuh wouldn't have got clear of that corral last night . . . I *was* hopin' you might have somethin' to suggest."

"What, for instance?" Ray flashed back scornfully. "That I told the rustlers they c'd use my corral, maybe?"

Pat saw that he would get nowhere with this man in his present aggressive mood. He shook his head slightly.

"Naturally, *I* don't know what you're up against," he said. "But you're not helpin' yourself any, boy, by talkin' that way."

Morgan's look was wicked. "Let me be the judge of that," he retorted uncompromisingly. "I don't know what your object was in helpin' me last night, Stevens—if that was yore real aim. It's yore own business. I won't bother to thank yuh, though, so don't count on it."

"Oh, that's all right. Candace has already thanked me—"

"She did it on her own, then. It don't mean anythin' to me!" Ray's tone was unyielding, resolute. Pat laughed ruefully. "You're a regular lone wolf, Morgan. Far as that goes, I approve of a young fellow goin' it on his own. Just make sure you don't stub your toe . . . And if yuh ever do land in a real jam," Pat added easily, "yuh might remember I helped you once."

"I might. But don't count on me," Morgan repeated.

Pat turned his bronc and started away, aware as he rode that the other was watching narrowly his every move. If he entertained any fears that Ray was capable of planting a slug between his shoulders, however, he need not have bothered. Glancing back just before passing from sight of the little swale, he saw Morgan once more wholly absorbed in the task of trying to save the bogged calf.

"I'd have helped anyone else finish that job," Pat mused, pushing on his way. "In Morgan's frame of mind, he'd have taken even that favor wrong."

Whatever it was that rode the young fellow's hump, already he was being driven to dire extremities. And perhaps he was fully justified. Pat was satisfied now that it was not Morgan who had shot at him. What, then, was the explanation of that unprovoked attack?

Pat hauled up at a sudden thought. "Maybe the same dose will be waitin' for Ray when he goes home," he soliloquized uneasily. But on second thought he dismissed the likelihood. Morgan had heard the shooting, for he had mentioned it; he could not remain altogether unwarned. Pat decided finally that the other could take his own chances. That, only too plainly, was the way he seemed to want it.

Half an hour later it was another matter when, after picking up the Star Cross trail and following it toward town, Pat presently described a rider coming toward him. He was not surprised, in another minute, to recognize Candace Cowan, mounted this morning astride a frisky sorrel mare.

Seeing Pat, the girl came on resolutely. At her approach, he pulled off his hat with a ready smile. "Now, I wonder where you could be goin'?" he opened up lightly.

Candace's answering smile was brief. "You've been to Ray's yourself, of course," she returned swiftly. "Is—everything all right?"

Pat assuredly did not intend to allow her to ride unsuspectingly into the Star Cross today, nor was he prepared yet to tell her precisely why. She already had sufficient cause for worry over young Morgan, and he did not propose to add more and worse to her burden.

"Too bad, Candace." He shook his head regretfully. "At least I can save yuh a longer ride. That boy's not home today. No use of yuh goin' on."

She weighed that in her direct way, trying to fathom its full meaning. "Perhaps he's somewhere out on the range," she said. "I must at least try to find him—"

Pat spread his hands. "No use. Ten to one he's taken fright, and is steerin' clear of Jess Lawlor for a day or two."

"No, Pat." She shook her head slowly and firmly. "That's not like Ray at all. I know. Wherever he's gone, some clear purpose has taken him." Her words were positive. "I'm certain he can't be far away as you imagine."

"Morgan *is* bullheaded." Pat affected to agree. "But *you*

ought to know what's got under his hide. It's plain something
has.'' He was confidential now. ''Some faint idea of what his
trouble is, might make it easier to help him—''

Candace understood perfectly what he was suggesting. Her
headshake was firm. ''You said last night you intended to
have a talk with Ray. I'd rather he told you whatever he
wishes to tell, Pat. That way, you may get more from him
than he's told me—which seems little enough,'' she could not
forbear adding.

Pat thought a minute, eyeing her absently. ''Oh, well. I
have seen him, Candace,'' he said finally. ''I may as well tell
yuh—''

''This morning?''

''Half an hour ago.'' Pat nodded. ''He never opened up at
all. Wouldn't spill a single thing. Probably feels he has just
as good reason to suspect me as anyone else!''

''But doesn't Ray understand how you helped him last
night?'' Candace burst out.

Pat shrugged. ''That don't mean a thing to Morgan. Or at
least he says so.''

''But that's ridiculous!'' The girl was plainly exasperated.
''I'll admit this much, Pat. Ray's convinced someone is
trying to ruin him—probably by driving him off the Star
Cross. But that he should imagine you to be in any way guilty
of such a purpose, simply doesn't make sense . . . Oh, dear!
Wrong-headedness won't cure his troubles. Wait till *I've* had
a talk with him!'' She started on.

''Wait up, now.'' Pat strove to block her, recalling the
rifleman lying in wait. ''I tell yuh Morgan ain't at the ranch—''

''No matter. I'll find him, Pat.'' Nor would she allow him
to accompany her a foot of the way, declaring her wish to
continue alone. After giving careful directions calculated to
lead the girl straight to Morgan, wide of the ranch house and
across the open range in comparative safety, Pat was forced
to let her go on.

4.

AFTERNOON SHADOWS LAY LONG and blue as two weary, slouching horsemen threaded the lonely pine canyons a dozen miles west of the wild Culebra Range. One sat his saddle tall and broad-shouldered, while the other, stout and stocky in butternut shirt and faded, bulging bib-overalls, rode with his stubby legs outthrust at what seemed a most uncomfortable angle. They were Ezra and Sam Sloan, the latter indulging monotonously in a querulous monologue.

"Danged if I know why I ever teamed up with yuh! It's a blazin' wonder we manage t' scrape together a decent livin', let alone get ahead," he complained acrimoniously. "Here we sell a sizable herd o' prime horses an' drive 'em close onto a hundred miles—with me doin' most o' the work. But *you* git t' carry the money! . . . Need it all for some shady poker debt, like as not, an' next time we settle our grocery bill it'll come outa my pocket!"

Ezra turned to examine Sam's moody face solicitously. "It's a question whether I can git yuh to the next town an' pour a drink or two into yuh, the shape you're in," he muttered doubtfully to himself. "I was afraid this trip'd be too hard, at yore advanced age—"

Animation sparked in Sam's lackluster eye as he fired up at this too thinly disguised form of sarcasm. "Go take a runnin' jump at yoreself," he roared. "I'm a right smart handful o' years younger'n you—ten, anyway, yuh superannuated hatrack!"

"My, my," murmured Ez admiringly. "Wastin' such high-class language on me! . . . Yuh musta spent a good ten years longer in kindergarten, too."

Sam scoffed. "I knowed more'n you the day I was born."
He broke off, his voice returning to normal with startling
abruptness for anyone who did not know these two. "How
much farther is it t' Ute Gap, anyhow?"

Ezra squinted unhurriedly at various landmarks looming
through the amber afternoon light. "Five miles. Mebby less,"
he grunted.

Sloan lifted his reins. "Let's set these boneracks a-clatterin'.
I wanta get home b'fore winter!"

As the little man said, the pair had just sold a herd of roan
horses at an advantageous price and had found it worthwhile
to make delivery in person. On the previous day they had
reached the isolated mountain ranch to which the animals
were consigned. A considerable amount of money had changed
hands, which Ezra had promptly appropriated and stowed
away, and after spending the night at the ranch, they were on
their way back to Powder Valley. Mending their pace in the
prospect of a pleasant evening at the high country cowtown,
they forged on.

Ute Gap was little more than a wide place in the road,
consisting of perhaps a score of odd buildings. Reaching the
place just as the sun was setting, they looked over the weathered collection of saloons, general stores, blacksmith shops
and sagging sheds, from the end of the street.

"Hope there's a place t' eat in this roarin' metropolis,"
Sam commented as they turned their mounts toward the
nearest hitch-rack.

Having dismounted, Ezra paused in the act of fastening his
reins and turned abruptly. "Hey, runt! Take a look at this—"
His thumb stabbed at the saddlehorse standing next along the
partially filled rack.

Sam craned to look. His prominent black eyes bugged out.
"What is that brand—? Star Cross!" His voice sank a full
octave. "Yuh mean young Morgan's here in town? So what.
We don't owe him nothin'."

Ezra shrugged. "Just so long as he don't git the idee we're
trailin' him around—"

"Wal! He can get over it again, if he does . . . Oh-oh!"
Sam broke off so suddenly that Ezra turned to look at him.
Over the back of his horse, Sam was peering down Ute

Gap's single street, his attention riveted on something. *"That* ain't Ray Morgan by a long shot," he muttered positively.

As he glanced that way, Ezra's gaunt face grew sober. He saw the man walking across the street a hundred yards below, his arm done up in a bandana-handkerchief sling.

His own tone was guarded. "What would Pike Tigart be doin' here?" He scratched his lean jaw thoughtfully. "By gravy, Sam, we've stumbled onto somethin' that looks mighty strange!"

For once Sloan was in thorough accord. "We lettin' it pass?" he queried. "Or shall we look into this—"

At another time Ezra would have brushed the matter aside with scant ceremony. But Pat Stevens's obtuse course of action where Morgan was concerned had piqued him.

"Why pass it up?" he grunted. He waited till the gnarled Flagg foreman was gone from sight, then spoke with energy. "C'mon. We're dragging' our broncs outa here 'fore them hombres so much as git a smell of 'em!"

Although he knew his hopes of a satisfactory supper and an expensive evening had gone glimmering, Sloan did not demur. He took time to slip into an adjacent store for a sack of crackers and a half-pound of cheese, and he and Ezra quietly retired to the cover of the pines.

Darkness soon fell. Stealing into Ute Gap on foot, the two were not long in discovering the men they sought. Oddly enough, although the grizzled partners did not find it strange, Tigart and young Morgan were together. Seated at a saloon table in a dusky corner, they appeared to be in conference. It was not possible to overhear what they were saying, nor could the watchers devise any means of accomplishing this; but the inferences to be drawn from a mere glimpse of the pair together seemed more than sufficient.

"Got over their differences fast enough, didn't they?" growled Sam when they had backed away from the window through which they had been peeping, into enveloping darkness.

"If they had any," Ez rejoined dourly. "From here it looks as if that fist-fight they pulled was a put-up job. Wouldn't wonder if Stevens'd be interested in this—"

"He'll hear about it," Sam promised.

They canvassed the idea of delaying to see more. It would have been a pleasure to both to shove undisputed proof of deep-dyed chicanery under Pat's nose, for their distrust of Ray Morgan was instinctive and strong. On the other hand, Ezra thought that, with haste, Stevens might be enabled to witness personally some part of the crookedness which they had little doubt was afoot.

After making the best of their way back to the horses, they carefully circled Ute Gap and struck out for the lonely trail over the Culebras. An early moon soon declining, darkness hampered their progress. At last they hauled up for the night, having reached the western slopes of the mountains.

Having crossed Aspen Pass in the high Culebras by mid-morning, they abandoned the circuitous downward wagon road for a more direct course toward Stevens's Lazy Mare spread. Working down through the foothills, they passed China Springs at no great distance. Ezra glanced that way more than once, his single eye slitted shrewdly. He finally spoke.

"Thought Stevens wasn't usin' his China Springs range this season—"

"He ain't." Sam drew rein long enough to peer down there through the intervening pines. "By grab, there's stock grazin' down there at that! I wonder . . ."

Both recalled how the rustled Lazy Mare steers had been watered at this remote spot. With a wordless exchange of glances, they turned their horses that way. Their approach was cautious, for it did not escape either that rustlers might even now be lying in wait.

Closing in on the isolated spring, however, they neither saw nor heard anyone about. At the same time, a surprise of another order awaited them.

"Hello!" Moving out into the open, Sam stared at the nearest steers, his normally placid face knotting in wrath. "Damned if Morgan's Star Cross stuff ain't moved in here. . . Look at that, Ez!"

There could be no mistake. Every steer in sight bore the distinctive Star Cross brand which had arrested their attention on the horse at Ute Gap.

Ezra's hard-breathing snort covered a wide range of expression. "That does it," he growled tersely. "Shall we git on t' Pat's an' dump this in his lap?"

Not often were the pair called on to cover ground with

greater speed than they exhibited in making for the headquarters of the Lazy Mare. Crusty Hodge was waiting for them on the porch, shading his old eyes with a wrinkled hand. He watched their hasty approach without visible emotion, and they knew him better than to expect a greeting.

"Stevens around?" Sam tossed out briskly, hauling up near the porch with a scattering of gravel.

Crusty grunted a negative, continuing to study them with some curiosity. Not for anything would he have asked a question, as a consequence making the best of what observation could tell him. They dismounted and thrust him aside bodily as they stumped into the kitchen.

"Okay—slap some hot grub on the table, an' make it fast!" Ezra bellowed, scowling at Hodge. "What yuh waitin' for?"

Knowing full well that his employer would acquiesce, Crusty reluctantly complied, in no hurry to accommodate them. Nor would he answer satisfactorily any of their gadfly queries concerning Stevens's movements today. Pat was somewhere about the ranch; that was all the saturnine handyman would vouchsafe.

"We'll have t' wait for him," Sam sighed. "I sure hope he don't ride in late—"

Pat's return was in fact early, for him. Jogging into the yard an hour before sundown, he grinned amiably at the two dour-faced old rawhides perched on the porch steps.

"Healthy-lookin' pair of old hellions yuh make," he commented inelegantly.

"Don't put that bronc away," Sloan sang out in laconic warning. "Yuh'll be needin' it!"

Pat tossed his reins to the ground, slid out of the hull and strode forward. He examined their faces with an interest almost equal to Crusty's own.

"What are you two doin' here?" he asked easily. "I thought yuh were away deliverin' some horses—"

"They're delivered." Sam lost no time in recounting what they had witnessed at Ute Gap, on their way home. "An' that ain't all, Stevens," he wound up. "Right now there's 'round a hundred head o' Star Cross steers grazin', big as life, on your China Springs range!"

Pat's mobile lips folded shut and he looked at Sloan slowly.

"Yuh don't say. There can't be no mistake about that, I don't suppose?"

"Mistake?" Sam flushed with indignation. "Hell, we seen 'em!"

Without more words, Pat turned to Crusty Hodge, watching them from the kitchen door. "Shove the grub on the back of the stove, Crusty," he instructed curtly. "We'll be havin' a late supper."

Taking the hint, Sloan and his gangling companion lost no time in reaching their horses. The trio singlefooted out of the yard and, once out on the open range, shoved their mounts to a brisk pace. Pat put a few brief inquiries as they made for China Springs, but for the most part he rode silent and thoughtful.

"I don't get it," he spoke up at last, shaking his head. "Star Cross stuff grazin' on my range, and yuh say young Morgan's way across the mountains in Ute Gap—or was?"

"You'll get it all right, once yuh take a gander," Sam retorted. "I know yuh ain't been able t' see what's right under yore nose, but mebby from here out yuh'll find it worth yore while t' look behind yuh!"

They batted it back and forth without getting anywhere and then, drawing near China Springs at last, fell silent and watchful once more. Pat was the first to open his lips, gazing down a long brushy slope toward the lush meadow surrounding the springs.

"Don't see any cows down there at all," he grunted, as if all along he had expected no other result of their ride.

Sloan's jaw dropped as he stared about suspiciously. It was a fact that no sign remained now of the steers he and Ezra had seen a matter of hours before.

"It's blame queer," he growled defensively. "The stuff cert'nly was here—"

As they jogged down the slope and drew near the springs Ezra attentively scanned the looming lava ledges which rose frowning beyond the little meadow. Suddenly he held up a hand.

"Listen!"

Faint sounds were indeed drifting from the direction of the ragged rocks. It was as if a considerable bunch of steers were being herded that way. Sam caught fire in a flash, slapping his fleshy thigh resoundingly.

"Uh-huh!" he exclaimed exultantly. "There yuh are, Stevens! Fifteen minutes later, an' we'd've been too late!"

Lifting their broncs into a run, they swept across the meadow and circled the ledges. The rough going here presently forced them to slacken pace, but the sounds of a cattle drive were unmistakable. A muffled cowboy yell pealed, and the bawl of a steer.

Five minutes later, in the fading light, they caught sight of the drive winding slowly across the broken malpais. One man was behind it, and as they closed in, Pat at least was not greatly astonished to learn that it was Ray Morgan himself.

"What's up, Morgan?" Pat waved a nonchalant hand as the busy redhead suddenly turned his head to flash a look backward.

Ray swiveled his bronc to face them squarely, holding himself tense and silently watchful. "Yuh want something, Stevens?" he said at last.

Pat was not inclined to be easy with him in the face of this uncompromising demeanor. "A civil word'll do," he returned dryly. "You'll grant my surprise to find yuh drivin' stock at this hour. Don't yuh ever quit?"

Morgan manifestly did not know how to receive this brand of cajolery. "When your stock strays, yuh drive it home. Or I do," he added succinctly.

Pat displayed mock astonishment. "You mean your whole herd strayed—in one direction?"

Even in this dim light Morgan's flush was noticeable. "I never drove my stuff down onto yore range, Stevens!" he protested earnestly. "Yuh can believe that or not, just as yuh like!"

"All right, Morgan. I'll buy it." Pat nodded. "As a matter of curiosity, though, how do yuh suppose they got there?"

Ray explored his serene features uncertainly. He shook his head at last, with a dogged expression. "I don't know. There's fine graze down there. And good water—"

"So yuh think maybe that enticed 'em, do yuh?"

Listening to this sparring exchange with dark, incredulous mien, at this point Sam turned to regard Ezra in scornful disgust. The lanky one returned his look with a shrug. Obvi-

ously neither of the pair placed any credence in a single word
the young rancher had to offer.

Observing them out of the corner of his eye, Pat spoke
with some sharpness. "All right, you two. It's no snap gettin'
a herd across these rocks with night comin' on. Suppose we
pitch in and get Morgan shoved along on his way?"

They stared at him unbelievingly. But Pat soon disillu-
sioned them as to his sincerity, turning to the work briskly
himself. With great reluctance they followed suit, and it
could only be said of them that at least they did their work
well. It was not yet dark by the time the treacherous malpais
was put behind the Star Cross beeves, and Morgan knew that
the worst of his troubles were over.

"You're a queer one, Stevens," he blurted out finally,
new energy in his tone. "Yuh had no call to lend me a
helpin' hand, but this time I'm thankin' yuh—and what's
more, I mean it. I'm plumb stubborn, I guess, but I hope I
ain't altogether a fool!"

"Nor a knave either, Morgan—or yuh wouldn't have been
in such a hurry to pull your stock back off another man's
range," Pat seconded, in smiling agreement.

"Not *that* kind of range, anyway," Morgan confessed
fervently, in a warmer tone than any he had used before. Pat
glanced at him curiously.

"You're thinkin' about winter range, I expect." His pause
was deliberate. "If yuh really need it, why don't yuh lease
China Springs, Morgan, and be done with it?"

Morgan shot a quick look at him, and then away. "Well,
now. If I only could—!"

"It's a matter of ready cash, eh?" Pat chuckled. "I know
what it is to get started, myself. Maybe we can make a deal,"
he suggested blandly. "Or wouldn't that appeal to yuh?"

Invincible wariness touched Morgan's stern young face
again. "Offhand, it don't. What is there I've got to offer yuh,
Stevens—that you'd want?"

"You can work, can't yuh?" Pat asked reasonably. "It
happens I'm a little short-handed right now. Help me comb
my Lazy Mare stuff down out of the breaks this fall, and your
winter range'll be paid for."

Morgan hung on the words hopefully. Yet still he delayed.
"How long'll that take, Stevens?"

Pat shrugged. "Matter of a week or ten days, I'd say. I won't aim to ask for blood in exchange for a little grass, if yuh get what I mean."

His disclaimer of sharp dealing was a shade elaborate, but he need not have bothered. A load seemed to have slipped off Morgan's capable back. He sat straighter, his freckle-dusted face brightening.

"It's a deal," he said. "I'm beginnin' to believe you're not against me, Stevens! I can't explain what I mean, but I'll take yuh up, an' return good measure into the bargain. Yuh won't be sorry for this!"

5.

ONE MORNING A WEEK LATER, having ridden to Dutch Springs from his ranch, Pat dismounted in front of Jeb Winters's place preparatory to stepping inside to the post office at the rear of the store. He had tied his reins and was about to enter the door when three rather boisterous young fellows burst out, one of them bumping into him roughly, and brushed past with little more than a grunt of impatience.

Pat paused in momentary surprise. The man in the lead he saw was Ray Morgan, whom, as it happened, he had not run into since their meeting at China Springs. Morgan saw him and gave him a boldly casual nod, far from conveying the friendly warmth he had showed on the previous occasion.

"How are yuh, Stevens," he tossed out coolly without breaking stride, much less offering to stop.

"Howdy, Morgan." Pat's response was equally indifferent, though he paused to glance after the man who had barged into him. He recognized the other instantly. It was Apache Lang, an unprepossessing adventurer with something of a reputation as a range tramp. The third man, Corny Miller, appeared no less unsavory.

Stevens watched the three stride away, making apparently for the Gold Eagle. His brows drew together in a frown. "What's Morgan's game, hangin' around with those hard-boiled Flagg punchers?" he asked himself uneasily.

There was, of course, the chance that their present employment was without significance. He had not forgotten Sam's story of Ray's conference with Pike Tigart, the Flagg foreman, at Ute Gap. Privately regarding that meeting as little more than an armed truce between the pair, Pat had shrugged it off. Had he after all made a mistake? This new development looked decidedly suspicious, to say the least.

Unless, indeed, it dated from an earlier time, Stevens was unable to devise any logical explanation of why Morgan should seek such an association. "He'll soon learn his mistake in runnin' with that bunch, if he keeps it up," he told himself.

It was not his headache, and he presently dismissed it from his mind. But that afternoon he heard that young Morgan and the Flagg men had been thrown out of a grog shop on the edge of town as public nuisances, and only the accident of Sheriff Lawlor's failure to catch up with them had saved the Star Cross man from being thrown into jail.

At least twice during the ensuing week, once from Sam Sloan's lips, it came to Pat's ears that Morgan had been seen hobnobbing with one or the other of the two Flagg riders, to the evident neglect of his own ranch work.

Meeting Ray one day alone on the street in Dutch Springs, he essayed a friendly, if smoothly veiled, warning.

"How's everythin' out at the Star Cross, Morgan?" he asked easily. "Boomin' along, I hope—"

The other, reading his intention instantly, returned a stony look which said that he would tolerate no interference in his affairs. "I'll be ready whenever yuh call on me, Stevens—if that's what you're drivin' at," he responded, with baffling obstinacy.

Pat waved a disposing hand. "Okay, boy. I'll let yuh know." He passed on his way without a backward look.

It was another matter one afternoon two days later when he met Candace Cowan on the trail half-a-mile from town. The girl replied to his hail with the briefest of greetings and would have driven hastily on had Pat not halted her discisively, struck by the forlorn look on her face and her air of depression.

"Wait a minute, Candace." Reining near, he propped a foot on the wheel of the flatbed she drove and peered into her eyes. "You've been cryin'," he said with concern. "What's that young rip been doin' to yuh now?"

"Nothing, Pat," she assured him with nervous vehemence. "Unless it's his inclination to take needlessly reckless chances. I'm afraid he's in serious trouble now—"

"Just come from town, didn't yuh?" He nodded in swift comprehension. "What's goin' on there?"

Her shrug was hopeless. "I'm not certain. I was—almost afraid to learn, Pat. George Haskell was throwing wild accusations when I came away, with Ray trying desperately to brush it all aside. I didn't want him to think I—that I—took it seriously . . . But how could I help doing that?"

Stevens patted her hand. "Easy does it, sister. I'll drift along and look into this." He smiled reassurance. "You've no idea how nosey I can get, when it suits."

She strove to brighten. "You've proven a real friend to him, Pat. This time I'm afraid—"

He waited for no more, but wheeled his pony and thrust on toward town. So Morgan had landed in a real jam at last, he reflected. Pat had suspected something of the sort, but he admitted to some curiosity concerning the actual source of the trouble.

A couple of dozen men were gathered before the Dutch Springs hotel, some of them standing on the porch, when he arrived. Ray Morgan and Jess Lawlor faced each other on the boardwalk, with George Haskell of the Rafter H scowling nearby.

"All I know is, my horse was gone—stolen right from that rack," the balding rancher was saying doggedly. "It wasn't *me* that seen Morgan leadin' a paint pony just like mine out of town at the very same time! It was Jake Ball, there—"

"What if I did?" Ball heckled, with short temper. "I still say it was Morgan I saw, an' the horse was a paint horse!"

"And I still say the horse belonged to Apache Lang, and he's in possession of it now!" Morgan's grating voice rose above the others', uncompromising and firm. He shot Lawlor a black look. "Find Lang, and see for yourself! But don't throw any horse-stealin' at me till you're dead sure, because I'll make somebody sweat."

"Wal, Haskell's hoss had disappeared, an' it's still gone," Lawlor spoke up with heavy finality. "Funny yore alibi ain't around now, Morgan. He's been underfoot often enough lately." He shook his head. "It looks bad for yuh, an' yore bad company is against yuh, too."

Pat glanced about. It was indeed significant that neither of

Morgan's questionable cronies should be in evidence in the hour of his dilemma. Ray affected not to see it that way.

"All talk, Sheriff—and mighty loose talk at that." He held his ground sturdily. "Nothing's hooked me up with this lifted bronc but Ball's blabber, and *he* hasn't identified the horse he saw me with. He can't! Until somebody can, an' makes it stick—" he snapped his fingers contemptuously—"yuh can all go whistle."

Lawlor's lean cheeks tightened, his eyes flashing. "So I can whistle, can I?" He appeared to be struggling in grim indecision, studying Morgan with disgust and growing resolution."

"Wal. After inquiries've been made, this can all be settled in my office," he growled finally. "Meanwhile yuh won't be goin' nowheres—"

Pat thought it time to step forward, his tone level. "That won't be necessary, Jess." He cut off Ray's angry explosion before it was launched. "I'm prepared to take him in custody till you've had time to decide just how bad yuh want him." He outlined the deal he had made with Morgan, to use his work as a rider in exchange for the winter range at China Springs. "I can use yuh now, Ray. Yuh said you'd stand ready to my call," he reminded.

Morgan flushed, appearing to find Pat's interference at this critical moment an impertinence. "Hang it, Stevens, I ain't knucklin' under to these buzzards—!"

Lawlor ignored him, peering at Pat hard. "I want to know! Yuh say you're handin' over yore China Springs feed, for two weeks' work?" His tone was brusque with suspicion. "It ain't like yuh, Stevens!"

Pat's cool demeanor failed to alter in the slightest. "Oh, the Lazy Mare manages to pay off . . . Do yuh trust Morgan in my hands, Jess?"

Lawlor scratched his head, undecided what to do. He beat down the vociferous protests of Haskell and others, not in the least impressed.

"Yuh heard Stevens," he threw at Ray sternly. "Will I find yuh where he says yore at, if I should happen to want yuh, Morgan?"

"Ain't makin' no promises." The young fellow had had a moment to think it over, however. "I told Stevens I'd work for him, an' that goes. But you and Haskell can take yore own chances, Lawlor. I'm no horsethief, and I won't listen to any such talk!''

More than one man in the crowd backed him audibly on this forthright stand. The lawman shrugged. ''Maybe Stevens can keep yuh in line, yuh bull-headed young fool,'' he exclaimed. ''If I do come after yuh, I'll get yuh!''

Jerking his chin down, he made a sign to Pat, plainly laying all responsibility in his hands, and turned away without more words. While Haskell and others milled about, arguing noisily, Pat was insistent and brisk.

''Where's your horse, Morgan? Get it up, and we'll drift.''

Ray would have protested, but a gesture silenced him. Pat was waiting for him by the time he climbed into the saddle. Men stared after them as they made for the edge of town; but George Haskell was not popular enough to enforce any open display of hostility.

Once in the open, Morgan jogged along moodily. ''I never stole his damn horse,'' he burst out violently.

Pat turned to him with a crooked grin. ''I only bargained for your work—remember?'' His tone was coolly aloof. ''If you've got any idea I'm worryin' about Haskell's troubles—or Lawlor's—forget it.'' He was silent for a moment. ''I made some reference to poor company once, and you shut me up. But maybe you've learnt your lesson. Now shall we put our minds on our work, Morgan?''

Swallowing his chagrin with some surprise, Ray could only nod.

After pausing briefly at the Lazy Mare, that afternoon they rode out to the hills together. For several hours Pat worked hard with Morgan, combing the mosshorns and strays down out of the upper range. The fall roundup was not many weeks away. The sky had grown tawny and streaked with clouds, the wind cold. Aspens had already turned to a blaze of gold, and cottonwood leaves were streaming across the open spaces in a steady rain.

Little or not opportunity for talk presented itself while they worked. When Pat led the way at dark to a well-stocked line cabin, neither felt like making conversation. They threw a hearty meal together, wolfed it down and tumbled into their blankets.

It was the same on the following day. Pat was pleased to observe that Morgan was a hard, efficient, relentless worker. But as day followed day and scarcely half a dozen words passed between them, he understood at last that Ray did not propose to volunteer any confidences whatever. He appeared not even to recognize the few openings offered to him.

"Reckon Lawlor's made up his mind he don't want yuh too much," Pat said on the third night, as they made for the line camp after a hard day. ' Maybe Haskell's bronc turned up in some unexpected quarter."

Morgan grunted, failing even to show curiosity about whether the animal had been located or not. "They know it won't do 'em any good to show up out here," was his sole comment.

Pat rolled that over in his easy way. "Think you were framed in that deal?" he asked casually.

Ray stared at him steadily. "Do yuh think anything else?" he rapped out tartly. "If yuh do, this is no place for me—"

"If I did," Pat rejoined without heat, "you wouldn't be here, boy."

It was their last word till they reached the line camp. Morgan went out of his way then to make amends. "Sorry if I snapped at you, Stevens," he got out with difficulty. "I'm kind of edgy, I guess."

Pat clapped him lightly on the shoulder. "Think nothin' of it, kid. We're both tired."

They talked cheerfully for a while, getting acquainted.

Sam Sloan rode in while they were eating. He peered at them owlishly from the door. "Thought I'd find yuh here—"

"Come in, Sam, and eat." Pat greeted his friend heartily, paying no attention to his suspicious scrutiny. Sharing their meal, Sloan confined his queries to their immediate work. He stayed for an hour and all too plainly would have liked to get Pat apart, but the latter gave him no opportunity.

"By the way, Sam." Stevens halted him as he was about to leave. "We've been stuck here several days now. Morgan's not said a word; but he'd like it a heap if you'd drop over to his place, say tomorrow, for a look around. How about it?"

Ray glanced up in surprise, and Sam caught the look in his eyes. He delayed for only a second.

"Sure, Pat. I'll do that—if yuh think it's worth while."

"I do." Pat nodded, saying no more.

Sam rode away shaking his head in dubious wonder. "Hanged if I savvy this," he muttered. "Pat's nursin' that bird like a good feller. Could it be he's watchin' his every move? Stevens can be shrewd when he wants."

The answer eluded him. But it was not in his book to refuse a favor when it was Pat who asked it. Protest and complain he might, but in the end he complied. He spent the night at the Lazy Mare, ordering Crusty Hodge around with a vengeance; and morning found him headed dutifully for the Star Cross.

The place was, of course, abandoned when he arrived. After nosing about curiously for some time, he found nothing to attract his notice. Except for short excursions across the adjacent range, however, he did not offer to leave. Pat's casual suggestion he interpreted as a request to keep a watch on the Star Cross, and this he meant to do.

The day dragged long and drearily, without anyone at all coming near the place, yet he continued to watch with care. Toward sundown his vigilance was at last rewarded when a lone horseman appeared, coming unhurriedly over the swells in the direction of the ranch.

Sam made sure he remained unseen, his horse out of sight, and was seated casually on Morgan's doorstep when the man jogged into the yard. His bushy brows lifted on suddenly recognizing the other. It was Mace Galloway, the iron-faced, thick-chested owner of the Flagg ranch.

Watching the other's advance without moving, Sam spoke at last. "Howdy, Galloway—"

"Hello, Sloan." It was not very enthusiastic. "Is Morgan around?"

"No, Mace, he ain't." Sam delayed over that one, his glance careful. "Somethin' yuh want of the boy?"

There was a dead opacity about Galloway's unwinking stare, though he appeared alert enough.

"What would you care?" he responded listlessly.

It was dropped arrogantly enough, and it brought all the man's offensive consciousness of power and importance into the air between them. Sam's thin lids did not so much as flicker.

"Why, I figgered if I could carry a message, it'd be an honor—"

"To you or me?" Galloway snapped cynically.

"I was thinkin' of you," drawled Sam as promptly. "It not occurin' t' me yuh wouldn't be interested—"

Galloway snorted softly. "Lippy party, ain't yuh?" he rasped harshly.

Sam was more puzzled than ever, seeking the reason for this active antagonism in a man he scarcely knew. Mace gave him no time to retort, but hauled his horse around and started away.

"I'll tell Morgan yuh called," Sam sang out. Galloway commenced to speak over his shoulder, thought better of it, and shoved on imperturbably. Long after he had passed from sight, Sam found himself still puzzling over the incident.

Ten minutes later he was himself in the saddle, racing across the hills. Pat and young Morgan were on the point of retiring at the Lazy Mare line camp when he arrived. Before them both he blurted out the occurrence at the Star Cross.

A moment's silence fell. Pat glanced at Ray. "It *does* sound funny . . . Know what Galloway may've wanted, Morgan?" he asked.

"No." The young fellow's negative was colorless. He did not even sound interested.

"Was he ever over there before?"

This time Morgan's delay was longer, but the answer was the same. "No, Stevens. He wasn't."

Pat thought about it in his unhurried way, then spread his hands. "Why not stay here tonight, Sam? We'll finish tomorrow, and Morgan can get on home—just in case Galloway should happen to stop back."

It was so arranged, although Ray remained singularly apathetic concerning the entire matter. Sam watched the pair curiously without learning anything whatever; and the following day, pitching in with them, he was too busy to indulge in any private observations. By midday they had finished the work Pat had laid out.

"That's it, Morgan," he said as they returned to camp. "Your China Springs rent is paid. Yuh can go home after we eat. Sam and I'll ride along and help drive your stock down there if yuh want—"

"Thanks, Stevens! I may've earned this—but, anyway, I'm damned obliged."

Any reservations Sam may have entertained as to Morgan's gratitude died on the spot. The young fellow was too obviously relieved and tickled for it to be less than genuine. On the way down to the Star Cross, Sloan asked himself if he had been wrong about this man.

It was another story when they arrived at Morgan's place. After spending a few minutes there, they were just leaving to gather his herd when they were met by an irate old man, driving his lathered bronc as if he would kill it and hauling in before them with a jerk.

"You, Morgan!" It was Zep Cowan, owner of the Bull's Head and Candace's father, and he was boiling with wrath. "Plannin' t' run off with my girl, are yuh? This is the second day she's been gone, an' I aim here an' now t' know what you've done with her!" One leathery hand was knotted tightly on his reins, and the other hovered clawlike over the cedar handle of his gun. Plainly he meant every word he said and was ready to enforce it at need. "Open yore trap, yuh two-timin' wolf—and yuh better talk fast!"

6.

Ezra would never have admitted to anyone, on the day Sam left him alone at the Bar ES, his reason for riding the high Culebra slopes overlooking Mace Galloway's huge Flagg ranch. Yet here he was, drifting along ghostlike under the towering spruce of the high levels and keeping a sharp eye peeled for anything likely to be of the slightest interest.

Beyond the vague conviction that a few men on this ranch had altogether too suspicious an interest in Ray Morgan's humble fortunes, Ezra could confess to no real reason for being here. Loneliness had set him to prowling restlessly, and sheer curiosity had done the rest.

For several hours he had observed nothing to arouse a deeper suspicion, nor did he particularly expect to. It was largely out of perversity that, spotting a lone rider far down the rolling slopes, he kept watch as the other laboriously advanced, climbing steadily. For long minutes Ezra lost touch as the tiny horseman entered some winding stretch of canyon or angled upward across a dense pine slope. As time passed he grew interested, wondering what errand might bring anyone into this remote area.

The time came when he thought he had lost his elusive quarry in a maze of wooded ravines. Circling hastily, careless of whatever racket he might make in the process, Ezra rode into the upper end of a tiny, parklike glade in time to meet the mysterious rider emerging at the lower end. Thus arrested, he sat his saddle rocklike, lanky jaw agape in astonishment on finding it to be a girl.

"I'll be danged!"

It was Candace Cowan, starting in cruel surprise at the totally unexpected sound of his harsh exclamation.

"Ezra! How in the world did you get here?" She quickly regained command of herself. "It wasn't particulary nice of you to track me so quietly—"

"Howdy, ma'am." Ez smoothly recovered his aplomb. "Wal now, yuh know I wouldn't've done that! It's pure accident, meetin' you. An' a right pleasant one at that." His smile fading, he pretended to scrutinize her with a new thought in mind. "What in creation would *you* be doin' way up here?"

Preoccupation dwelt in Candace's pretty features, despite her severity. Her thoughts were not hard to read. She had known this older man, friend of Pat Stevens and long an acquaintance of her father's, for years. Though he was homely as a mud fence and as unassuming, she found no reason for withholding her trust from him. Instinct alone persuaded her to delay and evade.

"I fancied I could find a more direct route to Pinetop, straight through these hills. It seems I'm not doing very well—"

"Pinetop." Ezra rolled that over on his tongue. It was one of the most distant and deserted cattle camps in a lonely country, lying so deep in the hills that few men were even certain of its exact location. "What in tarnation is the attraction up there?"

"It's Ray again, Ezra." She ignored his gruff astonishment, her words tumbling over one another now. "I learned this morning that he has met with an accident there. He— asked for me, and unfortunately he can't be moved." She strove to control her emotion. "That left only one thing to be done—"

"Pinetop!" Ezra repeated the name, not to be stampeded into any credulous extremity. "That's way to hell an' gone, yonder in the mountains, girl! Morgan's been workin' for Pat Stevens. The Lazy Mare range ain't in miles o' there."

"I know." She would brook no delay in which to reason the matter. "But Ray said they'd be climbing for strays . . . And I'm afraid he needs me—someone—badly!"

Ez shook his grizzled head dubiously. "Where'd yuh pick up this yarn?"

"Why—it was a line rider for Mr. Galloway, I believe. He was on his way for the doctor, and I didn't wait." Candace was frankly pleading now, her hazel eyes hurt by his disbelief. "Please, Ezra! This is all just a delay—"

"I won't be holdin' yuh up." Even Ezra's tone of concession could be dogged. "Fact is, I'm gonna make sure yuh git there."

The girl gave him a grateful look. "We must hurry," she exclaimed. "It isn't often that—Ray asks anything of me . . ."

"Yeh. Independent cuss." Ez nodded grim agreement. "I'd sure like t' know—" He broke off sharply. No point in letting her know that even now he doubted this excursion to be by Morgan's direct and express request. "Let's go. I'll lead yuh to Pinetop before yuh can say Jack Robinson."

That this was a gross exaggeration she did not need to be told. Afternoon came, and the sun dropped down the sky, with Ezra still leading the way onward.

He did not spare her or the horses. The air chilled rapidly as they climbed. The evening sky grew bleak. Snowcaps on the distant peaks glowed red in the slanting golden light and Candace shivered, drawing her jacket closer about her. From time to time her lanky guide shot her an appraising glance, but he uttered no word.

A tumble-down rock shanty at last appeared, nestled in a shallow cup between upthrust fangs of cold granite. Stunted pine dotted the ragged slopes, and the place had the most utterly forlorn air imaginable. The girl gasped.

"This is—Pinetop?"

"That's her." Ezra was busily scanning every inch of the lifeless terrain in sight.

"But there are no horses down there—"

"No." Ezra did not bother to glance again toward the deserted pole corral beyond the rock house. "Nor no hurt man inside nither, is my guess."

Candace turned numb and silent as it dawned on her for the first time that she had been deceived. Her lacerated feelings were balanced between honest relief that Ray Morgan should after all not be lying here gravely injured, and an uneasy doubt as to what it all meant.

Nothing was said as they rode down to the shanty, with its gaping slab door, and confirmed its total emptiness. Ezra was not long in determining that the place had not been tenanted for months, save by the badgers and rats.

Candace's gathering indignation expressed itself in a partially suppressed exclamation of impatience. "This is not very pleasant, Ezra," she said. "We can't hope to get home tonight—"

"Won't even try," he grunted. He looked about the cramped, untidy interior. "Nothin' t' eat here. But we can fight off the cold, anyhow."

Without fuss she resigned herself to the inevitable, well knowing it to be the only logical course. Hearing the faint crack of a gun while Ezra was out gathering wood, she rushed to the door apprehensively. The tall redhead was striding back, a knotty load of gnarled firewood over his shoulder and a limp coney in his hand.

"We'll have a snack," he announced with satisfaction. "There's a spring yonder, ma'am, if you're dry." He pointed it out.

Returning from a refreshingly icy wash-up in the fading light, Candace found a warming blaze awaiting her in the tumble-down fireplace, over which Ezra was already roasting the coney. Despite a lack of salt, her appetite was sharp set, the wild meat tasty.

Later Ezra made her comfortable on a fresh pine bough shakedown, with their meager blankets. "Git some rest," he advised. "I'll doze here an' keep the fire up."

Sure she would never sleep, her restless thoughts darting, the girl awoke suddenly in pitch darkness, startled to hear her big guardian moving about at the door. Evidently Ezra had heard some noise outside. He rasped the door open, letting the sharp air flow in, and stood peering out into the gloom. "Who's there?" His call pierced the windy night.

There was no response, and he moved outside, to be gone so long that Candace once more grew uneasy. He came stalking back, growling under his breath, and jammed the rickety door to once more.

"Did you hear someone out there, Ezra?" she asked.

"Thought I did." He was short of temper, as of speech. "It was them pesky coyotes, like as not, botherin' the broncs. Git back t' sleep, can't yuh?"

He built up the fire. Drowsiness stole over her again as she grew warm, and the next she knew it was freezing dawn, with golden early sunlight stealing through the chinks overhead. Ezra was stuffing sticks into the fireplace, wakeful and grumpy as if he had never allowed his head to nod.

Warming her fingers a last time at the blaze while Ez got up the horses, she was ready to leave. There was nothing to hold them here. Neither showed any disposition to talk as they jogged out of the little hollow, their breath and that of the horses showing in white plumes. Candace noticed her companion scanning the frosted ground keenly as if looking for tracks, but he offered no comment.

The biting chill stayed with them as they passed into thick stands of pine on their downward course. And then, quite suddenly, at a far lower level it was once more a mild and pleasant fall morning.

"I must thank you for looking after me, Ezra." Candace laughed to herself in a provoked way. "This might seem almost a pleasant experience, if it weren't so pointless—"

"Point to it, no fear," returned Ezra stolidly. "We jest don't git it yet."

The words brought back all her old uneasy doubts of the night before. "I shall certainly inquire into it deeper," she declared warmly. "Where are we going now?"

Ez shrugged. "The Star Cross is right in our way. We'll stop by, an' think it over from there."

It was not long past midday when they drew near Morgan's place. Unconsciously the girl looked forward with some eagerness. But it was Ezra whose keen eye spotted the four men grouped in a fold on the edge of the ranch, as if they had met their accidentally. Their voices had been high, coming over the brush; but they fell silent, turning to watch Ezra and the girl approach.

Recognizing her father and Ray at once, Candace brightened visibly. For her at least, all seemed right once more. She was thoroughly jolted when Cowan's dour lips parted in a forceful blast.

"Where yuh been?" he roared at his daughter in undisguised wrath.

Ezra appeared far less surprised than she, staring at Zep with unruffled calm. "Cool down, will yuh? She was told yuh'd had a fall from a hoss, up in the hills, Cowan," he averred evenly. "An' we went lookin' for yuh. Small wonder we didn't have no luck—"

Candace looked at this one-eyed prevaricator in surprise at his unblushing mention of her father as the man who had supposedly been injured. She understood his purpose, but had principle enough to disclaim any such protective evasions promptly.

"No, Father, it was—" she began.

Cowan gave her no chance to continue, but whirled angrily on Ray. "That's yore game is it, Morgan?" he bellowed, scarlet to the wethered folds of his stringy throat. "Tryin' to toll her away so yuh could run off with her! . . . I wouldn't put it past yuh to be in this, too, Stevens! I've heard plenty of yore slick doin's in the past." Manifestly he placed no confidence in any man present. "I ought t' have the law on yuh for this. An' what's more, I ain't sure I won't!"

"Daddy, please!" Candace broke into his tirade, distressed. Even Pat displayed a faint disgust.

"I expect it's easy to make allowances for your talk under the circumstances, Cowan," he said firmly. "You can't improve matters any by goin' too far."

"I'll go futher before I'm done!" the cattleman bawled. "Somebody'll scorch for playin' ducks an' drakes with my fam'ly. I won't have it!" He glowered at Morgan wickedly as if satisfied of that individual's role as the true culprit.

Ray listened to all this with gloomy resignation, saying no word and obviously wishing himself well out of it. Candace sent him a silently imploring message with her eyes and turned once more to her father.

"Will it do any good to swear these men had nothing whatever to do with my movements?" she asked stoutly. "None of them knew where I was going, or why—and I practically dragged Ezra along with me as it was—"

"No more! Not another word!" Cowan bit the order off intolerantly. "I can see as far through a shady piece of business as another man!"

"But Father, I tell you—"

"*I said dry up!*" he bellowed cholerically. "Get that bronc headed for home, girl, an' keep goin'!"

She saw how useless it was to prolong by a dozen words

this hopeless wrangle. Sorrowfully she turned her pony and started away. "Coming, Dad?" she called back.

Cowan halted his move to follow, scowling blackly at the men. "I ain't done with this," he warned them rigidly.

"Better walk a chalk line, all of yuh—or you won't be, neither!"

They watched him jog on, a stiff-backed martinet, to catch up with his daughter.

"Easy, Morgan," Pat broke the heavy silence to mutter. "There's plenty to explain here. But it'll pay to take that pair separate. Plenty of time, an' no need to rush it."

"Don't know whether there is time or not," Ray's tone was tight. "Better give us your story, Ezra," he rapped out harshly. "What's behind this?"

Ezra told what little he knew, addressing himself to Pat. They heard him out with attention.

"A Flagg line rider, eh?" Pat murmured ponderingly. "Who was it, do you know?"

"She didn't know his name." Ezra's second-hand description might have fitted a dozen men.

"That Flagg outfit again!" It was Sam who spoke, glancing at Ray. "They seem t' be hauntin' yuh for fair, Morgan—"

The other's expression was dogged. He said nothing, looking away.

"They wouldn't be tryin' their damnedest t' smash yuh, would they?" put in Ezra keenly.

"Why?" Morgan appeared to find this response unanswerable, as indeed at present it was.

They talked it over a few minutes longer, without his offering to contribute anything constructive to the discussion. Pat broke it up at last.

"You got out of this lucky, Morgan," he pronounced judicially. "At least we *know* you're not involved, an' that's solidly in your favor."

He noted the startled look on the faces of Ezra and Sam as the pair realized that what he said was true. Ray was off on his own tack, his lean young face hard and bitter.

"I'll bore the lowlife that started any crazy elopment story about me," he said sternly. "I'll find out who—an' that goes, right on up to Candace's dad himself!"

Pat's sour smile was unforced. "It's not a nice yarn," he

conceded. "But you'll think better of that ambition when you've had time to simmer down . . . Shall we get after those cows, and haze 'em along down to China Springs?"

It was a late hour, and they were ready to quit, when the task was accomplished. Whatever his twisted slant on other matters, there could be no questioning Morgan's genuine concern for the welfare of his little herd. He was effusive in his thanks.

"No, Morgan." Pat declined the young fellow's invitation to return to the Star Cross that night. "We'll drift along. Thanks all the same."

They parted a few minutes later, Sam and Ezra as indifferent as ever toward this man whose basic motives they were as yet unable to fathom. The fact was, as time passed they were finding Stevens's hidden purpose equally puzzling. That this nettled Sloan was apparent in his words when he finally spoke up.

"Hang it all, Pat," he burst out querulously. "Ever since Morgan come here yuh befriended him without a question—an' so far, it's brought yuh nothin' but grief!"

"Let's put it another way." Pat was indulgent. "It's Candace Cowan's judgment I've played along with so far—a level-headed little lady, if *I'm* any judge. *She* stands to lose the most, Sam, if it should prove that she's guessed wrong. Up to the present, I'm not prepared to agree that she has."

7.

CURIOUSLY ENOUGH, the few words of his exchange with Sam set Pat to thinking more seriously about Ray Morgan's tangled affairs than anything else that had yet occurred. Overnight he came up with various hardheaded conclusions, the validity of which he intended to test without further loss of time.

His opportunity came the following day, after he had ridden in to Dutch Springs. He had heard nothing of Sam and Ezra since taking leave of them the previous night, and it had been his hope that he might run into them this morning in town. But their horses were not to be seen anywhere along the street. However, as he was having his look, Pat spotted Morgan singlefooting in at the upper end of town.

Ray saw him. He lifted a hand, but might have ridden on by had not Stevens motioned to him. Morgan turned in at the nearest rack and dismounted to face the other diffidently.

"Morning, Red." Pat was genial. "Errand in town, I expect—"

Ray weighed that a moment, then nodded. "Yeh." He added nothing more, although Pat waited.

"I see." Pat's glance flashed across with sudden shrewdness. "Wouldn't be connected with—Sheriff Lawlor, would it, by any chance?"

Ray bristled, flushing. "What do yuh mean?" His tone was almost hostile. "*He* hasn't got anything on me that he can make stick. I thought we had that out!"

Pat met his eye levelly. "Morgan," he said abruptly. "It's time for a frank talk, don't you think?"

Ray made an attempt to maintain his bold front, but his evasive eyes betrayed him crawling back into his shell. His gruff reply was forced.

"Fire ahead—"

"How long's it been since yuh got out of Cañon City?"
Pat let him have it broadside.

In spite of himself, Ray's pupils leapt. "Wait a minute,
Stevens! What makes yuh think I've been in prison?"

His husky tone was a confession in itself. Pat only shrugged.
"Lawlor could find out for me, if you're bashful. It'll surprise me some if he doesn't already know." He regarded the
young fellow watchfully.

Morgan wilted. "Never mind. It's . . . true, Stevens." His
voice was so low that he could hardly be heard. "I was a
fool, an' I paid for it. But I swear I haven't done anythin'
wrong since I came to Powder Valley!"

"That's better." Pat's nod was serene. "I wouldn't be
here talkin' to yuh if I thought yuh had." He paused thoughtfully and glanced away. "What hold has Pike Tigart got over
yuh, Morgan—or whoever it is there on the Flagg outfit?" he
shot out.

Ray's careworn face hardened as he suddenly beheld the
chasm opening at his feet as a consequence of his simple
admission. That he was unprepared to go further was plain in
the bluster building up in his manner.

"Who says they've got any hold on me?" he growled
defensively. "I don't owe Galloway a thing—if you're thinkin'
of him. And that goes for the pack of 'em!"

"Which one did you meet in the pen?" Pat bored on.
"Was it Apache Lang—or that Miller character?"

Morgan hesitated while framing his reply. Before he spoke
Pat knew that, for better or worse, he had made up his mind
that concerning his own troubles his lips would remain closed.

"The hell with it." Ray was brusque. "My history's not
open to discussion, Stevens! What's past is over and done.
Lawlor, nor nobody else, 'll get anythin' on me because I
don't aim to pull anythin', in spite of the stories that's goin'
around. And that's where it ends. Is that clear?"

Pat's nod was deliberate. "Reckon I get your point. And as
far as it goes, you're well within your rights. But what yuh
don't see, Morgan—"

"I said the hell with it!" The Star Cross man was fierce.
"Yuh've been good to me, Stevens, and I ain't forgettin'.

But talk won't get us nowheres!'' With this final fling, he turned on his heel and stalked off.

Casting no more than a glance after him, Pat seated himself on a nearby porch step and thought it over. He had succeeded in verifying one shrewd intuition, and perhaps that was enough for one day. Naturally, having come out of the Cañon City prison recently enough to make it a still-painful memory, regardless of the reason for his sentence, Morgan was sensitive on the subject. In all probability he had since, as he averred, been going straight as a string. But what Pat feared most for him, Ray had not even allowed him to bring up—the certain danger inherent in resuming, for whatever purpose, any of the dubious associations formed in that unsavory place.

That Morgan was inexorably bent on settling his status with Sheriff Lawlor for once and all was made plain an hour later when Pat saw the stiff-shouldered young redhead march himself deliberately under Jess's nose. Pat wiped a grin off his mouth as he watched the dignified lawman's sour reaction to this performance.

''Red's daring him to make some crack about Haskell's horse, or try to take him into custody,'' he reflected. ''Can't help admirin' the young devil's grit, if it does seem sort of misplaced.''

Lawlor succeeded in ignoring the younger man's existence, and Ray moved on upstreet as if undecided what to do with himself. Even as Pat watched, he disappeared abruptly into a saddle and harness shop, and, looking around, Stevens was not particularly astonished to see Candace Cowan rolling along in her father's spring wagon.

The girl must have spied Ray, for she pulled up in front of the little store and waited. After some minutes' delay, Morgan stepped out of the place, much as if having reluctantly prepared himself to face the music. Pat paused curiously to observe the encounter.

From this distance the pair revealed little of what went on in their minds. Ray stood beside the front wheel, looking up, and Candace never took her eyes from his stern young face. Once she leaned toward him, speaking urgently. Ray stubbornly shook his head, waving a disposing hand. At last the girl half-rose, extending her own hand as if inviting aid. Morgan backed away, refusing to help her down.

"Young fool." Pat scowled to himself. "Candace wants 'em to be seen openly in town together. And she's right. No better way to kill ugly tales about him operatin' in the dark. But Morgan ain't agreein'. Probably he thinks this story about his bein' in Cañon City will soon get around, and that she's too good for him, anyway. He's dead right there—but shucks! That's true of us all."

He paused, watching as an indolent horseman came jogging up the street, turned in to the hitch-rail below the saddle shop, and hailed Morgan familiarly as he swung down. It was Corny Miller, the discredited and not very brainy Flagg puncher. To Pat's amazed disgust, Ray greeted the distraction as almost a relief, turning away from the girl with scant ceremony and moving forward to join Miller. Together the pair headed across the street for the Gold Eagle.

Candace set inert on the wagon seat for a minute or two as if dreaming. Pat read her sadness in the curve of her firm young shoulders. Then the straw-colored tresses tossed, and, lifting her reins, she drove on almost briskly. Pat briefly canvassed the notion of overtaking her, then shrugged it off. He moved leisurely toward the Gold Eagle, rolling a smoke with practiced fingers as he shoved through the batwing doors.

Miller and young Morgan were busily employed with artificial jollity at the bar. At least it was artificial on Ray's part, for his laugh rang hollow. Determining that they were intent on nothing more serious than killing time, Pat carried his drink to an unoccupied table and sat down.

Twenty minutes later Matt Kramer entered. His spread adjoined Pat's Lazy Mare on the north, and presently they were plunged into a discussion of range affairs. Sam Sloan put in a belated appearance, with his customery snaggle-toothed grin, and got into the talk.

"I hear Haskell's paint hoss was found driftin' loose down on the south range," Kramer offered.

"I heard that, too," grunted Sloan, noncommittally. "Reckon it got too hot for somebody t' hold—"

Talking it over, Pat found himself with little time for the sober cogitation he had planned; but beyond observing that Miller and young Ray had moved back to the pool tables, where they banged the balls about with the usual ineptness of rope-stiffened fingers, he paid small heed to the pair.

Kramer at length left, and the two friends sat for a few minutes in contemplative silence. Finally Sam jerked his head backward toward the men at the pool table.

"Right busy, huh?"

Pat knew he meant Morgan. "He's doin' a bigger job just now than yuh might expect—or so he thinks," was his grave response.

Sloan's brows jacked up incredulously. "You're a great guesser," he grunted. "What job'd that be?"

"He's trying to prove to Candace Cowan that he ain't worth a second thought—of hers, anyway."

Sam whistled soundlessly. "Looks like her old man's guff burned him up, there at the ranch—"

"No, that's not it." Pat spoke decidedly. "More like a severe attack of conscience, I'd say."

Head cocked to one side, Sam tried to figure that one out. But Stevens had stopped talking, on this topic at least; and all Sloan's disgruntled probing went for nought. Try as he would, he could draw no word from his taciturn friend to solve the mystery.

They moved across to the hotel for dinner and settled in the lobby afterward to wait for the arrival of the mail stage at two o'clock. It lacked yet ten or fifteen minutes of the hour, and they had temporarily exhausted all avenues of idle talk when a muffled gun crack echoed in through the open door from down the street, to be followed quickly by another and, after a brief pause, by yet a third.

Gunfire was by no means unheard of in this town at any hour. Sitting there, the two exchanged silent glances of casual inquiry. Sam started to voice a remark and then on impulse abruptly bounced to his feet and moved to the door for a glance outside.

It struck him at once that the street was ominously empty. Peering sharply, Sloan froze for a long second.

"That come from Jeb Winters's place, Stevens," he got out portentously. "Could be somethin' goin' on down there—"

Pat was at his shoulder, having his look. "Well." His tone was thoughtful. "Jeb's on a buyin' trip today, and Pop Branner's runnin' the place alone . . . We'll go down there."

The street remained silent and deserted as they strode forward. But in a matter of seconds it came to life. To Pat's eye, several horses racked before Winters's establishment appeared unwontedly restless, lifting their legs and yanking nervously at halters. They saw Sheriff Lawlor striding across the street unhurriedly, at an angle, making for the store porch.

Suddenly Jess ran forward, gun in hand, and grabbed at a man who attempted to duck out of the store too late. There was a sharp struggle. Lawlor hurled the man to the ground, kicking a Colt out of his grasp. A second later Jess hauled the fellow to his feet, more or less subdued.

At that juncture there came to Stevens's alert ear the quick thud of horse hooves around the corner. They pounded away in a twinkling. Sam ran toward the corner for a look, but he was too late. He came back shaking his head.

To the not very great surprise of anyone, it was Corny Miller, the no-longer swaggering Flagg puncher, whom Lawlor had collared. Jess shook him roughly, glaring into his face.

"What goes on here?" he barked. "Tyin' to pick up a little money the fast way, are yuh?"

Miller broke into a garbled protest which might be construed as a vehement denial.

"No, eh? Wal, we'll see. Get on into the store there!" Lawlor jerked him that way, hustling him to the door.

Immediately behind them, Pat peered around the lawman's stiffening back as he halted suddenly in the opening. He saw the extended legs stretched out on the floor, the toes pointing up. Craning farther, he glimpsed the man's rocky features, colorless now under the weathered bronze and without any signs of lingering life.

"Wal, dang me!" It was Sam who breathed the soft exclamation. "It's Apache Lang. Somebody let the wind outa him, neat an' complete!"

Forcing Miller ahead of him, his high-cheeked features turned to graven iron, Jess Lawlor stepped over the body and paused to cast a bleak scrutiny about the store. Old Pop Branner they saw seated on the floor, his thin back propped against a counter, chin on chest.

"Uh-huh!" The Sheriff was grim. "Finished the old man, too, did yuh?"

"Branner's breathin' yet," Sloan pointed out, stepping forward to examine him. "Got a slug through the shoulder, looks like.'' Gruffly he directed a cowboy standing in the door behind them to hurry for the doctor.

"The safe door's standing open," Pat announced. "And the mail sack's been dumped. They were after some steer money waiting to go out on the stage—"

Lawlor took it all in with fatal calm.

"All right, Miller." He was coldly curt. "You and Lang tried yore game on, and it looks like old Pop was too many for yuh. He cleaned Lang's clock, an' I reckon yuh winged him and then got rattled . . . Too bad I didn't ventilate *you* when yuh tried to run—"

"Yuh got it all dead wrong, Lawlor!" Corny chattered, looking ready to sink through the floor. "I was only standin' around here, mindin' my business, when the shootin' cut loose! I sear my only aim was t' git from under—"

"Oh, sure. For that matter, I reckon it still is," growled the lawman cynically.

"But I tell yuh it's true!" Miller was all but unstrung. "I dunno even if anything's gone—but as for findin' any stolen money on me, yuh never!"

"That's right, I didn't." Lawlor was regarding him narrowly. "Who was the hombre takin' off from in back of the store?" he rasped suddenly. "Like as not he was packin' the haul—"

Miller gaped at him. "In—back of the store?" he repeated stupidly, in a manifest play to gain time. He caught himself then. "I never saw nobody else, Lawlor," he insisted, too earnestly. "If yuh ain't dreamin', then it must be some natural mistake."

Jess pierced him with condemning eyes. "Mistake is right," slipped from his thin lips. "Meanwhile, where'd young Ray Morgan go—?"

"Oh, he left." Corny spoke with nervous haste. "I dunno where he's gone, Sheriff. But he—"

"Ain't in sight now." Lawlor nodded curt confirmation. "So I notice. Only, he was all mornin', an' up to a little while ago." He stared his contempt, never relinquishing an inch of his ground. "Why don't yuh come clean, Miller? . . . It *was* Morgan. An' he dusted when the goin' got hot." He delayed to lend point to his next words. "Yuh ain't makin' it a bit easier for yoreself by stallin', man! Yuh ain't gettin' away—an' we're sure to find out in the end."

Miller looked down at the floor, crestfallen, keeping his glance sedulously away from where the doctor worked busily over the unconscious Branner.

"Yeh. I guess that's right." He shrugged hopelessly. "Okay, Lawlor. Morgan was here. But he had no more t' do with this business than I did!"

Pat studied the puncher shrewdly. Miller's hesitations and his overpositive statements seemed exactly calculated to engender and strengthen those very suspicions against which he appeared to protest most eagerly. It was almost as though he were damning Ray Morgan by design. Stevens made note of the curious fact and filed it away.

Lawlor nodded sternly. "That's more like it," he encouraged gruffly. "Morgan *was* here, only he left sudden . . . Never mind why—" He lifted a beefy hand as Miller would have spoken further. "We'll take care of the details. Ray'll have his own story to tell when I lay hands on him! I don't think," he drawled, "it's goin' to pass muster, unless he decides to spill the beans right off." He seemed to have disposed of the subject for the present. "Let's go, Miller. I'm takin' yuh down to the jail."

"Better hunt me up a law shark, too, while you're about it," Corny muttered.

Sam moved over to Pat's side as the Marshal and his captive left the store. "This is bad, Stevens," he murmured. "I knowed Morgan'd git his foot caught in the crack. He would persist in foolin' around—"

Pat lifted his chin, not particularly worried, if his casual tone meant anything. "Don't forget this is Corny Miller's fine story you heard—and Lawlor's," he reminded Sam evenly. "Pop Branner will have something to say, when Doc snaps him out of it. Unless I miss my guess, what he knows should put a different face on the whole business, Sam."

Sloan glanced at him slowly. "Why, say!" he exclaimed guardedly. "Yuh may have an angle there—an' a smart one to boot! Wonder if Jess Lawlor's thought of *that* wrinkle?"

8.

Pop Branner came to after a while, displaying considerable weakness. It was mainly from loss of blood, Doc Barker pronouncing him to be in no particular danger, so long as he rested properly.

Under Pat's direction, with the medico in close attendance, several men moved Branner by means of a litter to the shack on the edge of town which he called home. Grumpy as a bear, the old man still was in no condition to talk. Most of his querulous grousing concerned Winters's store, left today in his charge.

"Slack away, Pop," Pat advised him mildly. "Sam's stayin' at the store to look after things. And Abe Kinney sent his clerk across to take care of the mail. Things'll be all right till Jeb gets back."

Branner would have had something to say about these arrangements, a hectic flush mantling his thin cheeks, but Barker shut him up with authoritative severity. "You'll talk when your time comes," he snapped. "The Lord Almighty couldn't stop yuh. As long as *I'm* the boss, Branner, you'll keep that trap closed!"

Pat left, grinning to himself. Returning to the street via a path alongside the hotel, he made it a point to show himself where men congregated. The story had, of course, spread rapidly over town, and there were many comments to be heard.

"Reckon Lawlor an' his deputy'll soon be bringin' Morgan in," Joe Casky, the bull-necked Dutch Springs blacksmith, remarked to Pat, pausing in his smoky doorway.

"Yes?" Pat was noncommittal.

Casky nodded importantly. "I had Rufe Dade's hoss here, ready t' tack on a new set o' shoes." Dade was Lawlor's long-faced gangling deputy. "Rufe come bustin' in jest now, an' yanked the bronc out in an awful sweat. 'Hold on, Dade,' I says to him. 'That an'mal ain't been shod yit. I had t' patch Luke Cagle's busted axle, an' couldn't get to 'im this mornin'—' Rufe never paid no mind. 'Shoes be damned! I need the bronc,' he rips out, an' away he went."

Pat let the man's garrulity flow over him for a few minutes, then walked away thoughtfully. It did not surprise him that Sheriff Lawlor was planning to pick up Ray Morgan at once. Rufe Dade could be leaving town thus hurriedly on no other errand. The fact lent urgency to Pat's own private plans, but he took time to walk back down to Winters's store for a word with Sam.

Stopped more than once by acquaintances who had heard he had been at the store very shortly after the holdup, he displayed little desire to exchange gossip, and a few minutes later stepped in at Jeb's doorway. Sam was pompously waiting on a few tobacco and grocery customers, but on Pat's appearance the little man waved him forward.

"These birds've already got Morgan convicted an' hung, Stevens." He lowered his voice to a hoarse whisper, gesturing toward the dozen or so townsmen and ranchers gathered before the mail window. "I never heard so much danged copycat, I told-yuh-so talk in all my life! Even that abduction yarn of old Cowan's is around—an' now they got Morgan in the doghouse for fair, with the door clapped shut. Funny part is, there ain't a one amongst 'em actually seen the boy leave town. It's enough t' make a man sick!"

Pat nodded. By no flick of an eyelash did he call attention to Sloan's abrupt change of heart toward Ray Morgan, but he understood. The young fellow's steadily worsening plight had at last reached a point where even Sam realized there was something decidedly fishy about it.

"Maybe we can fix that, Sam. I haven't given up all hope yet."

"Did Pop say anythin'?" Sloan asked, and he hung on the answer.

Pat was forced to shake a negative. "Doc shut him up like a feedbox till he's rested." He passed on the news gleaned from Casky, the blacksmith, and added, "No harm done if Morgan *is* back here in town when Branner talks. Either he's guilty as hell, or Pop's story could clear him altogether. And as far as Ray's concerned, that'll be so much gain."

"Wal." Sam mused over the situation unhappily. "Yuh better roost on old Pop like a mother hen, Stevens. I wouldn't accuse Lawlor of usin' a gag, but yuh never can tell."

Pat's assent was cursory. "Don't worry. I'm not overlookin' a bet."

He was about to turn away when Sam suddenly darted around the end of the counter, amazingly light on his feet despite his pudgy bulk. Turning, Pat saw Candace Cowan. There was a perceptible droop in her slim young frame, and those appealing hazel eyes looked defeated for once. She was pale as a ghost, but she had courage. She knew the story about Ray Morgan, understood thoroughly the buzzing whispers. Yet she braved the covert glances of these callous men.

Sloan officiously escorted her to the mail window, elbowing two or three men aside and all the while making gallantly audacious small talk calculated to advertise that, so far as he was concerned, nothing had gone wrong.

Stevens smiled and spoke, touching his hat. He could not help watching the girl with pity as she moved out, her mail clutched awkwardly in stiff fingers. Candace was crushed. Standing in the door, Pat saw her climb blindly into the spring wagon, while Sam busily handed up the lines, and start out for home like an automaton.

"Reckon she's licked," commented Sam gloomily, rejoining his friend. "I told her t' keep 'er shirt on—that we had a finger in this business, an' mebby Morgan wasn't completely washed up. She—seemed t' think you might be able t' do somethin'," he concluded apologetically.

Pat's smile was faint. Manifestly Sam found the prospect dubious, and he was forced to admit to himself that the chances were indeed slim. Without bothering to reply, he set off for Branner's shack.

Pop was asleep when he arrived, and the man who was looking after him shushed Pat with unnecessary loudness. Having his look, the latter settled himself to wait, squatting against the wall outside and smoking.

A lazy hour passed and became two. The dreamy afternoon

lengthened. Pat asked himself what luck Lawlor might be having in his search for Morgan, but it was too early yet to hear of any results in that direction. He yawned and settled himself more comfortably on his heels. A sudden roar, issuing from inside, announced abruptly that old Pop had awakened in no amiable mood. He wanted water, and subsided somewhat after allaying a raging thirst. His bitter eyes flared briefly on catching a glimpse of Pat.

"Waitin' around for the funeral, are yuh, Stevens?" he croaked testily. "Where in creation *is* ever'body?"

Pat's grin was dry. "Ease your halter, Pop. I don't think you'll kick the bucket in that mood. Yuh looking for Lawlor, or who?"

Branner muttered, pouting his toothless lips. "Wal, that sour-pussed Dade'll do in a pinch, but I want some law around here. I aim to git me some action, an' the sooner the quicker!"

Pat saw that he must humor the old codger if he was to get anything out of him. "Lawlor and Dade started out to pick Morgan up," he supplied casually. "They haven't come back yet. I'll notify Jess the minute he shows—"

"Morgan?" Pop snarled grumpily. "What do they want *him* for? Aim t' hand 'im a leather medal?" He shut up abruptly, observing the effect of his words.

Pat's ears pricked up in spite of himself. He masked his leaping hope. "Reckon you're the one who's in line for that," he laughed carelessly. "If it interests yuh, you turned in a pretty fair job of knockin' off Apache Lang. He was stone dead when we picked him up."

"Hell!" The old man winced at a twinge from his wound. "That was Morgan's valentine, Stevens. I never done it! Best *I* c'd do was t' make Miller drop his swag an' start runnin', before I passed out—"

A sack of loose coin and several registered letters had indeed been found partially concealed under the store safe, as if accidentally kicked there. It had not as yet been determined whether these were all the valuables involved in the holdup attempt or not.

"Lawlor grabbed Miller in the street," Pat informed.

"An' a good job, too, the ornery skunk!" exclaimed Pop

shrilly. "It was him drilled me! He made me mad, sneakin' in on me all alone, with a gun in his hand!"

Pat was calmly gathering the pieces of this queer story. "Where did Lang fit into the business?" he asked, deliberately pretending to misunderstand. "I don't see why Morgan ran, if he was backin' your play—"

"He wasn't too interested in neither side," said Branner, seemingly unaware of how completely he was being induced to divulge his story. "Seemed t' come as a complete surprise t' him . . . Corny Miller was diggin' in the safe, with a gun on me, when Lang shoved Morgan in through the front door. 'You're in this with us!' he says, an' Ray didn't like it a bit.

" 'You're breakin' yore neck t' pin somethin' on me, Lang!' he sings out. 'There must be somebody behind you that's mighty interested. I think it was *you* started this dirty kidnappin' story about me,' he says. Man, he was hot. One word led to another, an' Lang drawed on him. Morgan sure beat 'im to the punch, an' Lang dropped . . . That was my openin', right there." Branner paused for breath.

"Miller was so surprised, he forgot me for a second. I dived for Jeb's gun, layin' under the counter—an' I got it. Corny tried t' throw down on Morgan, divin' out the back door. He was too late. *I* got the slug." He scowled wryly. "Knocked me down, but I come up with a wobbly bead on Miller. Seemed t' scare him more'n if I'd knowed what I was doin'. He dropped whatever it was he was holdin', an' dodged out—"

The doctor came in at that moment. One look at Pop's flushed face, and he waved a preemptory hand. "All right, Stevens. Not another word, now," he rasped.

"Okay, Doc." Pat nodded. "I'm on my way."

He stepped outside and moved uptown with greater satisfaction than he had expected to feel. He had what he wanted. It was yet another hour before Lawlor came jogging in, minus his deputy. Pat got up off the bench in front of the adobe jail and stood waiting. The lawman stiffly dismounted, eyeing him silently.

"I take it you didn't locate Morgan?" Pat opened up.

"No. No luck." Jess's tone was colorless. "I left Dade at the Star Cross, in case he should drift back there. But it's my opinion the boy's headed for tall timber—"

"Maybe not." Pat's manner was mild. "I've had my ear to the ground, Lawlor, while you were gone."

Jess fixed him with a steady regard. "Old Branner, yuh mean?" he grunted, as if half-expecting what was to come.

Pat smiled. "We can't overlook the only impartial witness there in the store at the time," he reminded Lawlor gently. Without pulling his punches, he repeated Branner's story. Lawlor listened dourly to the end.

"Do yuh believe that yoreself?" he growled.

Pat showed astonishment. "Yuh mean you don't?"

The Sheriff shrugged. "I'll hear it from Pop myself," he said coolly. "And even then, I'll still want a talk with young Ray—"

"But, man, the thing's wrapped up!" Pat was almost vehement, mostly for effect. "This town's hounding Morgan already, without even allowin' him his day in court. But that ain't your style."

Lawlor was not to be talked around, however. "Facts interest me, Stevens, and nothin' else. Yuh may not know that Morgan's fresh out of Cañon City. In my mind, that has a direct bearin' on this case. Birds of that feather don't flock together accidental—an' till I know more, that's my last word."

Unable to get any more satisfaction out of him, Pat was forced to rest in the knowledge that justice appeared, at least, to be weighted in Morgan's favor. Moving up to the store, he learned that Jeb Winters had finally returned. In the process of checking the safe's contents, the merchant declared everything intact, unless later investigation disclosed some item of value missing from the mail.

"That lets Morgan out of the robbery end," Pat thought. "Lawlor'll be forced to admit that whatever he was there in the store for, Ray didn't pull out with any of the loot." He knew how far circumstance would go toward convincing the lawman that his original belief in Morgan's outlawry must be mistaken.

Ezra had ridden in, and Sam was busily posting his lanky friend on the day's events. They joined Pat, and all three retired to the Gold Eagle and talked it over. Ezra had not yet decided to espouse the young fellow's cause unreservedly—or so he chose to allow Sam to believe—and the situation was productive of considerable acrimonious debate.

As to Morgan's present whereabouts, they agreed that, as he saw it, he had sufficient cause to make himself scarce. Probably it would be difficult, if not possible, to run him down for a few days, until he had got over his initial scare, although on his way home that night, Stevens reached the conclusion that Pop Branner's straightforward story, once digested, would probably induce Sheriff Lawlor to pull away the guard he had shrewdly posted on the Star Cross.

The following day, work held Pat at the Lazy Mare. Roundup time had come at last, hastened by the weather. There were arrangements to be made, though Johnson, his silent and competent foreman, could be depended on to see the work through to a satisfactory conclusion.

At dawn the next day, heading for the roundup ground, on a sudden impulse Pat turned his horse's head in the direction of the Star Cross, intent on learning conditions there for himself. Morgan's ranch house was deserted as ever when he got there. Not even Rufe Dade was any longer in evidence. The deputy had contemptuously left Ray's kitchen door swinging wide on his departure, a gesture presumably motivated by malice; and there were signs that he had made free with the young fellow's food supplies. But that Lawlor had called his watch off appeared plain.

Pat delayed to clean up a bit, closed the place up tight and drifted out onto the range. It was inevitable that he should turn toward China Springs. In such a place, more or less cut off from the surrounding range, the little Star Cross herd might almost be expected to take care of itself. But knowing how things had been happening of late, he took nothing whatever for granted.

Only a few of Morgan's steers were in the immediate vicinity of the springs. But as Pat sat looking them over, there came a bawling of steers and clatter of cloven hoofs, and from the mouth of a wash several cows burst forth running, to join their fellows below.

Pat stared at the rider hazing them home and an incredulous grin split his lean bronze face. It was Candace, her straw-colored hair blowing from under the Stetson, perspiration beading her small determined chin.

"Well!" exclaimed Pat cheerfully. "Hanged if I know when I last met such a handsome puncher! And busy, too—"

Her answering laugh was provoked. "Don't poke fun at me, Pat! I've only been tryin' to hold Ray's little bunch together. It does seem that when the bellwether's away," she added ominously, "the wolves are sure to gather."

Pat nodded his comprehension. "Now that you mention it, I had the same idea," he confessed lightly. "This stuff's driftin' pretty wide, but I've a pretty fair notion where to look for most of it."

Together, under his direction, they hazed Morgan's stock back to the meadows without much trouble.

"Thank goodness the rustlers haven't yet thought of this unattended stock," the girl said, wiping the dust from her face with a kerchief. "Just how long it'll be before that happens, I'm afraid to think—"

"Be kind of interestin' to learn just where Ray's gone to," returned Pat.

"A long way, I fear."

"Maybe no," he argued. And then, after a pause, "Wonder if he knows he's more or less cleared of that business in Dutch Springs—?"

"I'm afraid it would make little difference, now," Candace rejoined sadly. She turned to him impulsively. "Pat, you've already done so much, I'm almost ashamed to add more to our debt. But you and I know that what Ray fears most is largely groundless . . . If you were to find him, couldn't you persuade him to come back regardless?"

He knew she referred to Morgan's supposed reputation as a jailbird, so bitterly oppressive to him. Arguing that out of existence might prove a chore to tax an angel, but Pat did not even mention it.

"There's the little matter of locatin' the young rip first," he told her practically. "It may take some doin,' but—" shrugging unconcernedly—"I can always try. And I'll do it for you, Candace."

9.

HERBERT CORYELL—COUNSELLOR AT LAW, the lettering on the door said. Beating a brisk tattoo on the panels, Pat wondered if the lawyer would be officially in at this hour, although it was known that he lived in a rear room.

After a delay a muffled call bade him enter. He swung the door back to find Coryell seated comfortably at the window, tieless, his sleeves rolled to his elbows, and thrust slightly forward in his chair, obviously having just removed his feet from the desk.

"Oh—you, Stevens?" Coryell was a thin, middle-aged man with permanently soured creases round his mouth. "Come in, come in," he growled irritably. "And shut that door."

Pat had known this man for a long time and, grinning with friendly warmth, was wholly untroubled by his bark.

"Howdy, Counsellor—"

Coryell drew his mouth down with distaste. "That damn sign," he said, in allusion to Pat's salutation. "I think I'd have it off the door—only the folks in this town'd forget me altogether."

"Listening to other people's troubles has made you pessimistic," Pat returned tolerantly. "Sorry to disappoint yuh this time. All I want is some valuable information I won't have to pay for."

Coryell waved vaguely. He liked Pat and occasionally shared his good humor, however sparingly. "I'll get it out of you in the end," he threatened. "What's stuck in your craw now?"

Pat squared himself in the most comfortable chair, his

smile fading. ''Just offhand, Herb, what do you know about the Flagg outfit, over here in the hills?''

''Not too much.'' Coryell's sleepy eyes alerted. ''Legitimate outfit on the face, anyway. Pay their bills, and sell cattle . . . Why? Don't tell me that Galloway's got into your pocket—''

''Not yet.'' Pat's headshake was minute. ''But he does interest me. Where'd Mace come here from, do yuh know?''

''Galloway? From over on the West Slope somewheres, in—in—What the devil is that name again?''

''Put your finger on it, man,'' Pat said disparagingly.

''Don't worry. I'll have it in a—'' Coryell snapped his fingers triumphantly. ''Bluestem Valley. That's it! Knew I'd heard the name somewhere.'' He sat forward suddenly. ''Stevens, I thought you were scoutin' around for young Morgan. What's this got to do with him?''

Pat did not bother to inquire how he had come by that piece of knowledge, nor did he waste any time sparring. ''I don't know,'' he answered honestly. ''I'm feelin' my way ahead like you do sometimes—such as you guessin' who I'm looking for . . . Do yuh reckon Galloway pulled out of Bluestem, lock, stock and barrel, when he drifted east?''

The lawyer rubbed his limber fingers together slowly and thoughtfully. ''I never handled a nickel of his business, Pat—''

''No matter. Things get around.''

Coryell nodded. ''Why—I understand he still has interests out there. I couldn't lay money on it. And what they amount to,'' he freely acknowledged, ''I haven't an idea.''

''That'll do.'' Pat stood up. ''Thanks, Herb, till you're better paid.''

Clumping down the steps to the street, he was in time to hail Ezra and Sam, riding into town this morning as they had agreed to do. Sam eyed him keenly, and was unusually short for him.

''This ain't findin' Morgan, Stevens—''

Pat was ready for him. ''You boys set for a ride?'' he countered briskly. ''A long one?''

They were all ears in an instant. Pat explained his lingering suspicions of Pike Tigart, the Flagg foreman, which they were well prepared to comprehend. He added what little he had learned concerning Mace Galloway's holdings, whatever they amounted to, in Bluestem Valley, miles over the mountains to the west.

"An' yuh figure we may locate Morgan hidin' over there?" Ezra interrupted.

Pat spread his hands. "I felt Morgan out about his tie-in with the Flagg bunch. He wouldn't say yes, and he wouldn't say no. All things considered, it's a chance."

They were inclined to agree. Accordingly, the three made for the Lazy Mare without loss of time and, after delaying only long enough to throw a pack on an extra horse, set out. Incorrigible adventurers as they were, they found zest in striking into the rough mountains stretching for more than a hundred miles between them and their objective, which had little direct connection with the probable outcome of their errand.

Evening found them far over the Culebras and approaching the little cowtown of Ute Gap. "It could be that Red's hidin' out over here," hazarded Sam.

"Keep an eye peeled for any Powder Valley people at all," Pat advised.

But riding boldly into the little street, their eyes busy, they saw no man with whom they could claim acquaintance. It suited Sam to haul up for a ready meal before pushing on; but the boarding-house served meals only at regular hours, and the cook was not interested in making any concessions.

It did not escape them that they were looked over with care in this town. At the only livery, Pat spoke casually to the unkempt hostler.

"We're headin' for Bluestem Valley, friend. Where's that lie from here, would yuh say?"

"Never heard of it, stranger." The man spat in the dust and turned away without interest.

"Keno," Sam grunted, regarding his companions sourly. "What'd yuh expect Red t' do—put up signs behind him?"

"If I did—" Pat smiled—"I'm wrong so far."

They pushed on before the curiosity of the town should be further awakened. After camping that night deep in the pines, they thrust on west and, on the third morning, having crossed the ragged Isabels, found themselves amongst the even more wild and imposing chasms of what Pat said was the Elk Range, looming ahead and mantled high up with snow.

"A divide up there lets us over into the White River country." He pointed. "Cloud Peak, in the Back Range, is our guide. I seem to remember Bluestem lies fairly close up under the peak. Maybe we can locate it."

A vast panorama opened out as they climbed the pass—for they were already at lofty plateau-level. Square miles of unbroken pine forest rimmed with flat-topped, nameless ranges spread to the south. They loved this untrammeled country next only to Powder Valley and looked long as they climbed, till the beetling shoulders of Badger Pass closed in on either hand. Snow clung in the rocky niches. Even the air was wintery.

"Sure rough an' ragged in here." Ezra waved a hand upward. "Great wonder the storms ain't loosened up them crazy walls an' tumbled 'em down."

The words were scarcely out of his mouth when, gazing upward in unison, they beheld a long section of hanging rock and rubble detach itself from the rim almost directly overhead, and start its wild plunge down the sheer slope. For an instant they stared in petrifaction. Then Pat hurled his horse forward, kicking the startled packhorse into motion.

"Get on up the trail!" Pat yelped. "We'll be smothered in here—smashed under tons of rock!"

The best speed they were able to whip up was no match for the onrushing avalanche. In a matter of seconds a heavy boulder bounded across the trail ten yards ahead of them, with a ground-shaking thud.

"We'll never make it!" Glaring back fiercely at that granite waterfall suspended above his head, Sam could barely be heard in the grinding, ominous rumble. *"This way! Come in here—quick!"* he screeched.

They saw him crowd his bronc- into a perilously narrow crevasse gashing the opposite wall. There was certainly no time to weigh contingencies. As Sam disappeared from sight, Ezra rushed in after him, cursing as the rock walls banged his bones. Kicking the balky packhorse forward, Pat was the last to rub through. He was only just in time, the crack of descending rubble mounting behind him to a thundering crescendo.

Thirty feet in, the passage curved and opened up slightly. Here, in the blue-gray light, he found his companions. Unable to crowd farther, for better or worse they were stuck here. "Get a cover over your face!" Pat called. By hoisting neckerchiefs over their mouths they sought to protect themselves against the heavy dust which billowed in like smoke, and they also managed makeshift tarp shields for the heaving horses.

The heavy, detonating roar went on interminably outside, deafening cracks mingling with sickening jars. The earth trembled. They dodged constantly as raw fragments of rock bounced about their heads in a steady rain. Gradually the tumult slackened. The dust grew worse if anything, Sam well nigh strangling as he choked and gagged.

The time came when only an occasional trickling of loose shale could be heard in the dead, somehow hollow silence. The dust thinned. Venturing to open his stinging eyes, Pat found difficulty at first in believing what he saw.

The crevice in which they had found haven had not been a foot too far from the trail. Indeed, it seemed a miracle that the avalanche had not rolled on a few yards more to fill the gully from side to side and bury them from sight of the sky forever. They had come that close to annihilation.

Pat stared up at the altered walls, a grave abstraction on his dust-caked face. "Did either of yuh imagine—" he began, only to break off.

"Huh?" Sam stopped coughing long enough to stare at him, red-faced. "Did we imagine what?"

Pat laughed carelessly. "I *thought* I heard a faint crack—just as that slide let go," he admitted.

Ez stiffened. "By Godfrey, yuh did! An' so did I," he blurted. "It was a gun-shot, Stevens! . . . Somebody turned that mess loose on us!"

Sloan gazed at them, his jaw clamping shut. "He musta knowed that cliff almighty well, t' know where t' shoot. Mebby he had a key prop picked out . . . It *could* be done with a pair o' glasses."

None thought it worthwhile to discuss what should be done about it. Silently they set about climbing out of the rough gully, closed now at both ends. It took management to extricate the horses from the jagged rubble, and the pack animal was found to have sustained a broken leg. Ez pulled out his gun and wiped the dust from its working parts, but Pat halted him.

"Leave it," he said tersely. "No sense advertisin' our-selves. We'll come back this way."

Unemcumbered, they led their mounts laboriously up the long slope opposite to that on which the slide had occurred. A tortuous canyon gash enabled them to surmount the soaring crest. They worked out onto a pine plateau seemingly isolated from the lower world, the ancient piñon trunks marching away not unlike cathedral aisles. Snow had fallen up here, melting banks lying in the chill shade; yet the grass was emerald, and there was the curious odor and freshness of spring.

"Listen!" Ezra held up a hand. When they paused, there came to their ears the faint monotonous bleating and hub-bub that could only mean sheep.

Putting their horses in motion they raced down the long slant through the trees, making no sound on the century-old, springy pine-needle mat underfoot. A break in the forest gave place to a luxuriant mountain park; and a quarter mile across, bold against the sky and the ragged pine-spired horizon, a lone sheep herder looked out over his flock.

They jogged that way, ignoring the tail-wagging dog that loped forward, free as a swallow, their eyes fastened on the stalwart herder, who glanced in their direction once and then away, stolidly awaiting their approach.

"Hey, you José!" Sloan called gruffly.

The Mexican eyed them inscrutably, missing nothing. A bronze image, he did not appear interested in anything about them.

"What yuh know about that slide?" Sam hurled at him, waving back toward the canyon.

The man stared a second, shrugged, and shifted his rifle. "No savvy," he growled. Yet the air up here still carried a faint golden haze of dust, and the slide must have been audible for a dozen miles at least. He could hardly have remained in total ignorance of what had occurred.

Pat threw curt questions at him in Spanish and pinned

down the grudging answers, but the results remained meager. The herder had heard a rumble, but had paid no heed. He knew nothing, had simply continued to guard his charges— the only occupation for which he was paid.

"Anybody up here with yuh?" Pat demanded unrelentingly. The answer was no.

"Find his camp," Pat growled. "We'll settle this."

They had no immediate luck, and it was the jealous dog that unwittingly led them to it, barking as they worked through the scrub growth not far away. Situated in a little hollow near high ground, the camp was both simple and eloquent. It was perfectly plain that two men had been living here for some time.

They were making this not-unexpected discovery when a rifle slug whined over their heads. Sam, snarling his disgust, plunged to cover in the hollow. "Shall we take him apart?"

"That wasn't that herder." Pat was quick. "It must be our busy friend! We'll corner him for a little talk—"

"It'll take some doin,' up on this mountain," averred Sam.

But Pat had noted that the plateau top was not overlarge, and fairly regular in shape. "Slip down the wash," he directed. "We'll string out across the mesa, an' have him penned at one end. Work him toward a corner, an' he's ours."

It was not without braving the menace of flying lead that they spread their cordon, but it was presently accomplished. At Pat's signal they worked north through the pines, away from the sheep. Ezra blocked an escape attempt past his flank by the rifleman, exposing himself to a hot barrage and sending back a hotter one. The quarry knew what was happening to him. Soon he would grow desperate. It was Pat who first clearly glimpsed the fellow, already on foot, and tossed a sizzling slug at him.

"Throw down your gun!" Pat called. "Give it up, or this is your finish!"

The answer was a ball that sang past his head. The man was game, but they had him cornered close now. They dismounted and pushed through the solemn pines in which a keen wind whispered. It became step-by-step progress, with less than a thousand square yards of cover remaining in which a man could hide. Strung out, the three friends kept each other continually in sight as they closed the trap. Suddenly glancing upward, Pat let out a chesty yell.

"Look out, Sam! Over your head!"

Sam thrashed around and darted a look up through the boughs of the gnarled pine directly overhead. He glimpsed a faint shape there, and a flicker of foreign color.

Two guns crashed flatly, his and that other. A slug slammed into the ground beside Sloan. Lying there on his shoulderblades, glaring up, he watched as the marksman cached in the pine slowly doubled in a knot and came crashing down, to land with a sodden thump.

Closing in warily, they looked the man over. He was an unshaken range hand, tough and unprepossing, and they had never seen him before. Now he was dead.

"Had t' to it," growled Sam apologetically.

Pat's grin was more of a grimace. "Nobody's kickin'," he said. "But there's no answers there—"

"Wal." Ezra grew sententious. "His boss'll carry out pack, if we did git it the hard way."

They located the horse after some searching and turned back. The Mexican herder was now gone from sight, and they let it go, hurriedly sliding down into the pass for their pack, putting Pat's injured horse out of its misery, and shoving on. Night caught them in cold country, but the morrow saw them across a wide valley of golden aspens and drawing near the Back Range, without having glimpsed another human being.

They climbed a long pine ridge before dark, only to find more tumbled crests beyond, a tangled wilderness. Pat shrugged. "Bluestem's up in here somewhere. Maybe a few miles farther along."

They had venison for supper, and morning saw them on their way, grumpy with the cold. Toward midday, with Cloud Peak piercing the sky almost overhead and dominating all this iron world, Pat hauled in on a low divide and pointed.

"There she is, boys," he grunted. "Bluestem Valley. Mace Galloway's home range must lie down there somewhere in the folds. And what a range!"

For miles below them, stretching along endlessly under the menacing, black-shouldered peak, countless acres of the best upland range in western Colorado lay open to their gaze, lush in mountain bluestem and threaded with winding creeks.

But as they looked, it became gradually evident that something was wrong. For no cattle strewed the slopes down there, no comfortable ranch sprawled on an overlooking rise. Bluestem Valley stretched desolate and bare, as empty of life as if it had lain thus for a thousand years.

10.

"SHUCKS! THIS CAN'T BE Bluesteam at all." Thus Sam Sloan, gazing about, voiced his disappointment. "Yuh got yer ropes tangled, Stevens. We'll have t' hunt further'n this for any line on Galloway worth havin'—"

Pat weighed his reply without haste. It did seem a queer setup, far different from anything he had expected, but he had no idea whatever of giving up. "We'll go on further—but not lookin' for Bluestem," he said with quiet firmness. "Like it or not, Sam, this *is* the place we're looking for. No mistake about its bein' bare as a board, either. Our next move's to look for the explanation."

Sloan grumbled, if Ezra did succeed in holding his peace. Neither tendered any active objection to riding down into the valley for a look around, idle as it seemed.

It was at first not greatly different from wandering into a prehistoric, uninhabited world, even the black rock ledges which broke the long rolling sweeps of gray sage wearing a most desolate look. Blue quail flushed out of the brush, running more often than flying; a lizard darted here and there over the sun-blasted rocks, and a mile in the sky, an eagle swam in lazy circles.

Pat noted Ezra glancing after the coveys of quail in some perplexity. "Well," he said. "What about it, Ez?"

The lanky tracker shrugged. "Mebby nothin'," he allowed. "But them birds're commonest after cattle's been usin' a range." He went on studying the weathered ground and a few minutes later growled triumphantly. "Thought so! Here's old cow tracks, Pat. Can't be more'n a season old, an' likely less—"

While the others had their look, he traced out further evidences of stock grazing. Manifestly cattle in considerable numbers had gathered on this range at one time or another.

"We'll just trace the direction of movement along the valley," Pat said. "Must be some point where these wanderin' trails run together. It may tell us somethin'."

Early afternoon saw them working into a main trail. Here the furrowed lines of extensive travel gave testimony to a considerable stock movement over a period of time, some of it fairly recent.

"Dangd if this don't look—" began Sam tentatively.

Ezra broke in on his words to point toward a pile of rocks, half-concealed in a coulee, about which there lingered some faint appearance of design.

"Say, that's a rock hut," Sam took him up, peering. "Must be intended for rough weather use, an' not much else. Let's take ourselves a look."

They found it to be little more than a makeshift bear den, mouldy and rat-infested, its roof sodded. Dried-brush shake-downs lay in the sagging bunks, unused for weeks, and a leather shoeheel and one or two rusted cans lay about.

"That cooks it," exclaimed Sam gruffly. "This is a station on the Outlaw Trail, Stevens! I thought as much when I seen that trail, an' now there can't be no mistake!"

Pat stepped outside and glanced away over the hazed sage swells and slopes of delicate columbine. "It may explain why Bluestem's never been consistently ranched," he soliloquized. "One range in a thousand—but a little too handy to the lone wolves."

"An' jest what do yuh make of Mace Galloway havin' 'interests' in this country, Stevens?" Ezra demanded shrewdly.

Pat's grin turned wry. "Well, it hasn't escaped me that those interests might—just possibly—have some close connection with the Wild Bunch. It's plain Mace is not runnin' any feeders out here; and we'll have to look elsewhere for his outfit, if he's got one in this locality."

All were aware that they were trading on pretty thin clues. It was only Lawyer Coryell's say-so that the Flagg rancher had any present connection whatever with Bluestem Valley. The hint had seemed worth while tracking down, and—

especially after what had happened to them at Badger Pass—it still did.

"Where's the nearest town from here?" Ezra asked.

Pat was uncertain. "It might be Mesa, over on White River."

"More like Redstone, up here in the Sawatch country," the one-eyed giant hazarded. "Mesa must be all o' forty mile—"

"You may be right at that. Shouldn't wonder if you are," agreed Pat, understanding at once Ezra's reason for asking. "Mesa's on the wagon trails, too. Redstone'll be more what we're looking for."

"Let's git goin', then," Sam seconded. "No tellin' how long yuh'd wait here for somebody t' come along."

They set out, guiding themselves mainly by the compass of the ranges, the lofty peaks being the only certain landmarks in this outflung world. The three had visited Redstone once before, some years ago, and its location was not altogether forgotten.

It proved rather closer than expected to Bluestem Valley, however, being little more than a matter of twenty-odd miles. The slanting rays of the great red sun sliding down into the murky west yet lighted their course when Pat said the little back-country cowtown was not far off.

"Reckon there's any harm in showin' ourselves in Redstone?" inquired Sam. "Because if that *should* turn out t' be Galloway's headquarters—"

Pat got his point. He had already been considering the matter. "The hope is that it will prove to be the hangout for his bunch, of course," he returned. "We won't deliberately advertise ourselves—but we'll have to ride in there, if we aim to look the place over good. It'll be a case of duck if we spot anyone we know too well; and from there on, we'll have to take our chances."

In the interests of prudence, they accordingly pulled up a half-mile from town and waited for dusk. Gradually the chilly evening lowered, spreading its yellow, lonely light over the range. At last Pat said they could push on.

Redstone was only a double row of wooden structures, many of unpeeled logs, stretched out on a flat beyond the cottonwood clumps marking the course of Blanco Creek. Because of its isolation here, the supply stores were unusually large. They were for the most part closed at this hour. A sprinkling of dim lights marked the great number of saloons.

"Bigger'n some burgs I've rode into, a whole lot closer t' Denver," Ezra grunted as they looked the place over from the edge of the street.

"Serves a mighty widespread area—in somewhat skimpy fashion," assented Pat. "Tough, too. I doubt if there's even an accredited marshal here—"

"No," Sam seconded. "These merchants know a big share o' their trade comes from up an' down the Owlhoot Trail. They won't risk drivin' that away."

"Must have t' stand their own chances o' gittin' robbed occasional," commented Ezra.

"It happens, I expect." Pat was not giving the topic much thought. "But it's to the Wild Bunch's own interest to see to it that renegade outlaws aren't allowed to spoil a good thing."

After leaving their broncs at a shadowy barn, the trio strolled upstreet. Redstone was surprisingly well-populated and busy. Men glanced at them sharply in the faint light from the saloons, but they were not accosted. They had their drink at one of the less popular bars, and continued to nose around. It appeared, however, an investigation without result, and they felt themselves pretty much against a blank wall.

"Reckon we wouldn't have no luck locatin' Morgan in this hive, if he *was* here," groused Sam as they surveyed the darkened street without hope. A jangle of tinny music assailed their ears, and there was a mild hubbub of men and horses moving about. "Looks like yer whole guess turned out t' be dead wrong, Stevens, an' time-consumin' into the bargain!"

"I wouldn't say so." Pat's gaze was fixed as he spoke. "Take a gander over there, old boy, and see if that interests yuh—"

Glancing over his pudgy shoulder, Sam stiffened. A group of horsemen were riding sedately down the street, closely bunched and murmuring amongst themselves, as if perfectly confident in this remote setting. At their head, eyes turning neither right nor left, rode Pike Tigart, the gnarled Flagg foreman, his arm still suspended in a loose sling.

Moving back into shadow, Pat and the partners watched this bold cavalcade advance. They appeared to be well known, being hailed from various points; and the raised hands and casual glances of their acknowledgments said that they were conscious of power and prestige.

"Wal, now!" Ezra breathed as a soft clatter of hoofs carried the men on by. "This is somethin' like. I didn't know Tigart was roddin' a rough-barked bunch way out here. It sure looks as if he was ready for business!"

"We watchin' this?" muttered Sam guardedly, shoving away from the wall.

Pat was tersely dry. 'What would you suggest?"

But they had barely begun to drift down the street, with a view to seeing where Tigart's outfit were headed for, when Ez sank a bony elbow into Sam's midriff with such violence as almost to deprive the stocky little man of speech or breath.

"Catch that—yonder," the big redhead almost hissed, indicating the direction with a jerk of his prominent chin.

Pat got a glimpse of Ray Morgan, staring after Tigart at the same time that he appeared to cling to a porch pole, next which he stood, for such cover as it afforded. A moment later he moved on, gliding through the dense shadows.

Turning to his companions, Ezra laughed soundlessly. "We've tracked down the young scoundrel. Ain't no doubt about what's on his mind, neither—"

"If he hadn't been so concerned about Tigart," Pat assented, "I don't know how he could've missed seeing us. He must have passed us inside of ten feet, and never so much as suspected it."

"We'll jest watch him for a spell, anyhow," growled Sam, rubbing his ribs after Ezra's poke. "But gimme another jab like that, beanpole, an' I'll slug yuh one!"

They pushed on circumspectly, keeping Morgan's tense silhouette in sight. Tigart's crowd, it presently developed, had dismounted farther up the street before a kind of tent pavilion in a vacant lot. Three or four coal-oil flares lit the smoky interior after a fashion, the doors looped back; but outside, the place was gloomy and somewhat brush-cluttered. Young Morgan was taking advantage of this fact to draw close.

Pat saw that the tent amounted to a gambling den, apparently newly opened, with a plank bar across one end. It was well patronized. Inside, Pike Tigart moved about, speaking familiarly to jostling men and stopping to confer with professional gamblers, his manner one of authority.

"Hang it, Pat—he's runnin' this place!" muttered Sam in some surprise. "Could it be for himself—?"

"Or Galloway." Pat nodded. He was beginning to comprehend at last the shadowy nature of the Flagg rancher's holdings in this country and would have liked to know more, but they prudently hung back in order to avoid stampeding Morgan, who hung around one of the doors, peeping in undecidedly.

Tigart they could still see through the ropy layers of smoke, taking everything in with masterful aplomb. At a wave of his hand a tipsy cowboy was given the bum's rush, and the crowd laughed briefly. Tigart turned then toward a rear door. The canvas flap swung, rustling back in place behind him, and after a delay, a tall, hard-faced man followed.

Morgan saw this also. Stepping back, he melted into the shadows.

"Must be an office tent in back," Ez murmured. "An' Morgan's figgerin' t' listen in—"

Automatically they followed suit by circling deeper into the brush. The faint light from the street did not penetrate this far, and there was only a faint starshine to take its place. It was enough, as they cautiously proceeded, to show them a hunched form beside one wall of a smaller tent in the rear of the establishment.

"We oughta grab Morgan—'fore he disappears," Sam whispered.

"No, not yet," Pat breathed in warning. "Let him listen a while. He may catch something good."

The moments dragged by while they marked time. If Morgan moved at all it was to work closer.

That Sam had been thinking hard was made plain by his next low-toned observation. "We'll never be able t' grab that boy where he is now. It'll be a dead giveaway, with Tigart jest inside— even if he ain't tryin' t' hear nothin'."

Ezra snorted softly. "I'll fix that. Yuh want 'im now?" He turned inquiringly to Pat.

The latter hesitated. They dared not delay too long, he realized. To lose track of Ray now would be a great mistake; and he was sure to run, once conscious of detection—and perhaps surer yet, were he to guess their identity.

"Okay—but play it smart."

Ezra proceeded by rustling the brush smartly. He had Morgan's attention almost at once, for the young fellow crouched lower and seemed to be looking around.

"That's it," Pat was grimly amused. "Again, Ez—"

The brush crackled faintly. Next moment, the wary Star Cross man responded by starting to crawl away. They were ready for him, lyin in wait where he must pass, a short distance from the corner of the big tent.

Ray was nothing if not cautious, proceeding a few feet, then halting to test his surroundings. Pat delayed till it was too late for the other to make a dash of it. Then abruptly rising out of the brush, directly in Morgan's path, he spoke up guardedly.

"Morgan—"

The thoroughly startled man scarcely reacted according to expectation. With a deep-reaching gasp he ducked and ran straight at Pat, at the final instant dodging sidewise and attempting to plunge past.

Had Pat been alone, the maneuver would have succeeded. It was foiled by Sam and Ezra promptly leaping on him from either side. The three collapsed in a heap, almost knocking Stevens off his feet. But Ray was not done yet by any means. He struggled fiercely, thrashing about in something like desperation. It was largely by long practice that the partners were able to presently to subdue his wiry strength and agility, pinning him down, aided to an extent by Pat.

"Get him away from here," the latter panted, glancing about them. "I don't know if we were heard or not—"

They hauled Morgan toward the rear of the lot, where the brush was thicker and comparatively undisturbed. Again Ray summoned every ounce of strength in a wild effort to break free, but it was useless.

"Ray," Pat rapped out, to fix his attention. "Cut it short, will yuh? It's me, Stevens."

The words did not immediately penetrate Ray's understanding, for he continued to wrestle about. But on their repetition, he broke off his exertions abruptly.

"Huh?" There was bafflement in his grating voice. "Stevens, yuh say?" He stared hard at them all. "An' this is Sloan and Ezra, no doubt—" Little enough relief sounded in the words. "No matter! Leggo—both of yuh! I don't know what you're grabbin' me for, but I got no particular interest in learnin' . . . Turn me loose, an' be quick about it!"

11.

"TAKE A REEF IN YOUR LEAD HALTER, Morgan, an' calm down,"
Pat advised with some sharpness. "Since when have we done
anythin' worse than lend yuh a helpin' hand?"

Still and alert, Ray seemed to be searching for flaws in this
argument. "I've got no written guarantees from any of yuh,"
he growled defensively. "You could be Powder Valley
deputies—from all I've heard, you've acted that way in the
past—and I can't think of a better reason right now for your
comin' so far. Yuh ain't takin' me back!"

Sam snorted explosively at this obdurate stand, and Pat
shook his head impatiently.

"You couldn't be more wrong, boy. Give us credit for an
innocently selfish object once in a while, can't yuh?"

Morgan stared. "Yuh tellin' me you ain't interested in my
movements—after grabbin' me this way?"

"If you mean, are we interested in makin' you go anywheres
yuh don't want to go, no," Pat assured him. "I doubt if
you're even wanted in Powder Valley, as a matter of fact. I didn't
bother to inquire before I come away, but I got the impression
Sheriff Lawlor had decided to leave well enough alone—"

Ray took a deep breath. "How could *he* know what actually happened there—or any of yuh?" he demanded, husky
with hope.

"You're forgettin' old Pop Branner," Ezra told him, grinning. "Miller got Pop in the shoulder, but he c'd still talk.
Have t' shoot his chin off t' stop him from doin' that. An'
Pop knowed who was stickin' him up, an' who wasn't, and
don't yuh forgit it!"

Morgan caught at that like a drowning man, "Go on, Ez,"
he urged. "Give me the rest of it!"

"Hold on," Pat interposed. "There's plenty to be told, all right, but let's get out of Tigart's back yard here, before somebody stumbles over us . . . Ain't there someplace where we can stick the coffeepot on an' chew the rag?"

Ray's reply was a concession. "I've got a camp in the cottonwoods, a mile down the creek," he offered. "No danger of bein' overheard there—"

Sam handed back the gun he had wrenched from Morgan's holster. "Sorry we had to rough yuh up," he said, "but we couldn't let yuh run before yuh knowed why yuh was doin' it."

Ray chuckled grimly, "I'm not delayin' any these days for explanations, that's a fact."

After circling quietly, they picked up their mounts from the dark barn while Morgan fetched his own, and once they were together again, the latter led the way out onto the flat. After a time the faint dark silhouette of low hills rose against the paler sky. Morgan slowed.

"There's a bank here," he warned. "Better lead your broncs down."

They slid downward to find themselves on a bench of the creek bottom, shrouded by young cottonwoods and cluttered with thick brush, well screened from observation by anyone who was not familiar with the spot. At a tiny clearing Morgan fumbled about, kneeling, and presently a tongue of flame leapt up.

"That's better," Sloan grunted as the fire came to life. "These nights're gettin' chilly on the fingers."

"Stuff 'em back in yer pockets, where they generally are," Ezra retorted unfeelingly.

The big fellow staked the horses and then broke out the blackened coffeepot carried in their pack, filling it at the creek and propping it in the blaze. They gathered about in prop-heeled ease, chafing their hands before the flame.

"Suppose yuh let me have old Branner's yarn," Morgan proposed finally.

Pat accommodated as tersely as he knew how. "There's only a few facts missin', Ray, from the story as it reached Jess Lawlor's ears—and those only you can supply. With them, he won't have much choice but to clear you entirely." He squinted curiously across the fire at the Star Cross man. "Yuh *can* supply 'em, of course—"

Morgan was nodding abstractedly, as if memory were busy in him, "I can, all right, Stevens, if it's any of Lawlor's affair."

"It'll be about Cañon City, I expect." Pat nodded to himself. "Jess already knows, Morgan, It's happened, and yuh can't change that. Better come clean with him."

Ray assented reluctantly. "Anyway, you fellows know that Miller and Apache Lang were actually behind the business. I met 'em in the pen, Stevens, and we got pretty well acquainted. They took it for granted I was their kind—and when they found out different, they decided to force me into their game."

"I've got a pretty fair idea how far that deal went," Pat said quietly. "It would seem pretty fantastic if a man *didn't* know."

Morgan gave him a quick look, swallowing hard. "It would've been fantastic," he agreed, "if yuh didn't get what was behind it. I figured it out finally that Pike Tigart was tellin' them two what to do—either for his own purposes, or actin· under orders."

"That's a shrewd point," Pat broke in. "Tigart is Mace Galloway's right bower, I take it . . . It *is* Galloway who's behind that gamblin' tent here in Redstone, isn't it?"

"It must be, Stevens. Tiggart wouldn't have the money." Ray was reasonably positive. "I know he's been here—Galloway, I mean. He just isn't the kind to allow Pike to run a business of his own—or anyone else, if *he* can grab the profit."

"So yuh were tryin' to tie Tigart up to the rustlin', or whatever's goin' on." Pat's tone was careless. "Is that it, Ray?"

"He's certainly mixed up with them owlhoots," Morgan declared. "I've long been sure of that—"

"So that's what yuh were doin' with Tigart there at Ute Gap," exclaimed Sam unguardedly. "We thought—"

Ray froze up in a flash. "Saw me with him there, did yuh?" he rasped. "So what *did* yuh think?"

Ezra's grin was disarming. "We thought yuh was playin' his game, boy," he said flatly. "Reckon that's what yuh wanted him t' think, too! Small wonder if we didn't savvy the play."

Morgan subsided slowly. "Yes, I was tryin' to work him for information. He couldn't prevent it, while he was trying his damnedest to drag me in deeper."

"How much did yuh get, listenin' there at his tent just now?" Pat inserted casually.

Morgan shook his head. "There was some deal cookin', Stevens. I couldn't figure out just what. That hombre Tigart was talkin' to isn't a Powder Valley man, an' most of the talk went clean over my head. I'll bet anythin' it was crooked as a mesquite fence—but what it concerned, I couldn't gather."

Pat was not surprised. "I wouldn't have thought you could get that close to Pike to hear anything at all," he said. "Don't he and Galloway know you're out here now?"

Ray shrugged. "I'm not quite that stupid. They must suspect as much, knowin' I've pulled my freight away from the ranch . . . Just how much they're prepared to let me find out, of course, I couldn't say, and I haven't waited for anyone to tell me."

"So jest what do you know?" Sam thrust at him.

"I know there's a stock trail straight out here from Powder Valley," Ray flashed. "And a station or two along the way. The Flagg outfit knows all the wrinkles, too. I learned that much."

Ezra and Pat exchanged glances. "Sure. That's where all yer Lazy Mare stuff was goin'," the redhead growled. "At least till the day we stopped that bunch above China Springs—"

"Usin' my range—and my corral." Morgan nodded unemotionally. "Tigart was behind all that, Stevens, breakin' his neck to tie me in."

"So you're returnin' the compliment." Sam grinned.

"It's self-defense, Sloan! *I* know how impossible it is to get out from under the tar brush in this country! Tigart knows too, damn him! Give a dog a bad name, an' cross him off the list. That's Tigart's scheme . . . Do yuh blame me for bein' scared too death?"

Pat shook his head decidedly. "It takes brains to be scared at the right things, boy. Your mistake was figurin' it's already too late."

Ray stilled. "How'd yuh figure that out?"

Stevens waved a hand. "I've watched yuh tryin' to brush Candace Cowan off," he said bluntly. "Do yuh know what she's doin' right now—or was, when we left?"

Morgan didn't, and Pat told him.

"She was workin' away all alone, out there at China Springs, Morgan, tryin' to hold your outfit together. Not because anybody asked her to, but because she thought it was the right thing. That's how much she thinks of you! . . . If yuh aim to get a girl like that—and they don't come any finer—you'll have to deserve her."

Morgan gulped, "I know, Stevens. I wish she'd—" He couldn't finish it. He didn't really wish she'd forget him, and they both knew it.

Pat led the talk to lighter topics, and they were still sipping their steaming coffee when a rattling of gravel sounded from the bank at the edge of the bench. Faint but unmistakable, it heralded the arrival of a horse.

Ezra sprang up, a lanky figure of alert concern; and even Pat and Sam looked quickly toward Morgan. He alone remained unperturbed, unless to stiffen slightly. Although it could only have been from expectation, he did not so much as glance about him in the darkness.

There was a soft thud of hoofs drawing close and a coolly ironic voice came to them from out of the shadows. "Thought yuh'd welcome a visitor or two, Morgan. But I notice you're already purty well supplied—"

"Get down, Euchre," Ray returned quietly. "Always room for a few more, yuh know."

Three shadowy figures drifted up in a semicircle, to sit their horses unmoving. Glancing up at the blocky, expressionless faces, Pat had little difficulty in placing these newcomers accurately enough. They were outlaws, or men lingering on the fringes of outlaw activities—as were most of the hard-featured riders to be encountered in this country.

Obviously the leader, the one called Euchre, stared at Pat and his friends with bold insolence. "Don't believe I've met these hombres—"

"Oh, that's all right." Sam was in his glory in such a situation, "We're easy t' meet. Rest yore saddle, Euchre—or go on about yore business, whichever pleases yuh most!"

That Euchre was not unacquainted with this brand of straight-from-the-shoulder talk, and even expected it, was plain from his casual reaction. He simply ignored it, fastening a leaden regard on Morgan.

"Yuh ain't talkin', Ray," he pointed out softly.

Ray roused himself, faintly surprised. "Why, these boys are friends of mine, Euchre," he said hastily. "I knew a lot of folks 'fore I met you. What's got into yuh?"

Euchre eased his seat in the saddle without replying. Thus far his two companions had not opened their mouths to say anything. Studying the cagey trio narrowly, Pat thought he had little trouble in placing them. They were free riders whom Morgan had somehow scraped acquaintance with since coming to this range, and it seemed extremely unlikely they had any connection with the Flagg outfit. On the contrary, it seemed more probable that they were no particular cronies of Tigart or Galloway and might even be aiding Morgan in his investigation of the two. Pat took his cue from this likelihood.

"Euchre's playin' it safe, Morgan," he observed with dry amusement. "It wouldn't be that *he* don't like the Powder Valley crowd much either, would it?"

The cool owlhoot pinned him with a knifelike glance. "What would yore handle be, friend?"

"It might be Sheriff Lawlor," Pat drawled. "If that's the kind of a name yuh go for—"

"Easy, Pat," cautioned Ray, a little hurriedly. "Don't forget we're all sittin' ducks here. No point of antagonizin' Euchre more'n there's any need to."

Pat laughed lazily. "Euchre and his friends would've been dead ducks by this time if I had any interest in it," he asserted flatly. "We might as well understand each other while we're about it . . . But I haven't got ambition enough right now just to back up a brag. What's all this about, anyhow?"

From Pat's rocky tone and the raffish appearance of his partners, who watched every faintest movement about them with flat, attentive eyes, Euchre had already more or less concluded them to be an outlaw team in their own right. But he was bent on making sure.

"Jest look over the brands on their broncs, will yuh, Bent," he said to one of his companions.

Nobody said anything as the man stumbled toward the picketed animals. "Two bar EMs, one Flyin' Hencoop, an' a Quarter Circle R," he called back gruffy.

Sam Sloan began to laugh. "Put that way, it might tell yuh somethin', or it might not—" he began.

"Hold it." Cracking like a blacksnake whip, Pat's ringing voice cut in. Over this thigh the dully glinting barrel of his Colt was trained squarely on Euchre's vest. "Suppose you take a look at *their* brands, Ez," he barked. "I never was one to leave a job half-finished. Who knows but what Euchre might be sheriff of Redstone, travellin' in disguise?"

Ezra relished this task, rising to comply with gangling indolence. He took his time. "Looks like two Barred Winders, an' a Turtle on a Rock, near's I kin make out," he vouchsafed. "Anythin' else yuh wanta know, Stevens? . . . Shall I look at their teeth?"

"Okay." Pat tossed his weapon into the air spinning and caught it adeptly and thrust it into the holster. "Now that we're satisfied about each other, shall we try a little target practice—?"

He did not appear to care what the answer would be, but Euchre had had enough of his horseplay. "I'm willin' t' agree now yuh got private business, Morgan," he said gruffly. "We'll mebby see yuh later—"

Pat waited while the outlaws unhurriedly turned their horses and pulled out. "Just who are your new friends, Ray?" he queried softly.

Ray was obviously embarrassed. "I met 'em in a bar, Stevens, and I'm not fooled any about what they are. But they was square with me," he said stoutly.

Pat watched him struggle with the words, then smiled. "Oh, *I'm* not above usin' whatever tool comes ready to hand, myself," he said assuringly. "Euchre must've been givin' yuh a lift along, wasn't he?"

"He—showed me around Bluestem Valley," Morgan acknowledged. "Not that there was much to see."

"Sure." Pat was serene. "And right now he's wonderin' exactly who we are, and just how much yuh might've talked . . . Well, he can set his mind at rest, an' so can you. If we all never opened our lips to the crooks and bad eggs, Morgan, this would be a lonely world."

His eye strayed to Sam and Ezra irresistibly as he concluded. Sloan's hackles began at once to rise.

"Suppose yuh jest make it clear what you mean by that last, Stevens!" he brought out truculently.

Spreading his hands, Pat winked at Ray. "You see what a guilty conscience can do for yuh," he whispered with exaggerated secretiveness. "All those two've got to do is hear the word crook mentioned somewhere in the next county, an' they turn around and yell, 'I am not!' at the top of their voices."

Morgan laughed a little distractedly. "That's really aimed to me, I suppose," he said ruefully. "Not that I blame yuh a lot. but I'm learnin' fast." He broke off, stirring the fire thoughtfully. "What's the next move, Stevens?"

"Well, I no longer approve of this place overmuch, for some reason," Pat said practically. "It's too apt to prove popular—and don't forget that Tigart's got the money at his command to pay for information in this country." He put a few more terse questions, probing the extent of Morgan's knowledge.

"It's plain enough that Redstone is an outlaw hangout," he summed up finally. "But not where they do their fast work . . . I'm in favor of headin' back for Bluestem without much loss of time. Now that we know plenty does go on out there, we can afford to wait a day or two for it."

"Yuh mean you'll—help me get the deadwood on Tigart and his crew?" Ray found it hard to go on. "It's me that stands to gain from this deal if I can jam it through, Stevens. I don't need to remind yuh—"

Ezra and Sam laughed at him. "A steer off o' Pat Stevens's range is jest as expensive as any, boy," Sloan scoffed. "Jest do yore own share t' help us pin down these long-ridin' gazebos, an' we'll make out t' collect our own profit one way or 'nother."

Morgan, more than content to let it stand that way, turned to get up his horse.

12.

STARS POWDERED THE VELVET SKY with shining points of light
as they pulled away from the creek bottom. The night air was
still, layers of biting cold lying in the hollows. Blanco Creek
was several miles behind, the dull glow of Redstone no
longer visible in the sky, when they hauled up in a thick,
protective stand of firs topping a low ridge. A matter of ten
minutes saw them rolled in their blankets, the fire burning
low.

Bleak, orange-tinged dawn, stinging cold, promised a fine
day. Ezra and Sam hopped about awkwardly, stomping into
their boots, and it was Ray Morgan who had the morning fire
going in a jiffy, while Pat threw breakfast together. Hot food
made them all feel better. The sun had scarcely lifted above
the low horizon, round and red, when they rode out of the firs
and struck off briskly for Bluestem Valley.

"Whut yuh aimin' t' look for over there?" Ezra asked,
drawing his skimpy vest closer about his lank frame.

"Don't know." Pat spoke briefly. "That's what we're
ridin' over there to see, Ez."

"There might not be anythin' doin' now till way next
spring," Sam pointed out, with gloomy morning pessimism.

Pat shrugged, "Could be. But with roundup season on, it's
my guess there'll be plenty of action—that is, if Mace Galloway and Company are in the business I think they are."

Young Morgan appeared more cheerful today, brightening
considerably at any word addressed to him and displaying a
willingness to bandy rough jests with Sam and Ez. For the
first time it was clear that he had accepted the three friends

unreservedly. At Pat's prompting, he grew voluble on the subject of his ambitious plans for the little Star Cross ranch. The first real property he had ever been able to call his own, though still conspicuously modest in extent, it began to assume dignity and importance in his talk. Recent bitter experience had begun perceptibly to mature him, as well; almost the only thing that had power to excite him was some open threat to the security of his little holding. That such a threat actively existed at present none of his auditors sought to deny.

"But why should them hombres be pickin' on me, anyway?" Ray wondered, in profound perplexity. "I never did a thing to 'em!"

"That ain't the point, Ray." Pat was thoughtful. "For operations of the size he's undertakin', Galloway needs tough, dependable men. And good men for his work don't grow on bushes. He figures you to be a natural, after Cañon City, and he's not leavin' any stone unturned in his effort to recruit yuh. Once he's got the goods on yuh, you're his man, like it or not—and Mace knows it."

Morgan nodded unwillingly. "An offer to work for Flagg did come to my ears," he admitted. "That was some weeks ago. I never gave it a thought . . . It could be the reason that Galloway showed up at the Star Cross, the day Sam was there."

"Sure. Mace was follerin' his offer up," agreed Sam. "I seen he didn't cotton to it when I got curious. An' he sure wouldn't talk."

"Reckon he savvies you're wise to his game now," Ezra put in. "A whole lot depends on jest how bold Mister Galloway figgers he can git. Better watch him close from here out, boy."

It was wasted advice so far as Morgan was concerned. In his talks with these men, which had opened his eyes wide to a number of things he already strongly suspected, he had reached the firm conclusion that Mace Galloway, outwardly affable, well respected in Powder Valley, and comfortably beyond normal suspicion, was in reality his mortal enemy.

"He won't get anywheres with me," he promised dryly. "I never did shine up to his oily ways. But from now on he'd better forget I'm livin'—or be mighty sorry he remembered!"

"We're all on to him now. But from here out that won't be enough," Pat reminded Morgan gravely. "I've run into Galloway's kind before. It's the rock yuh won't see comin' that'll most likely hit yuh in the back of the head."

Ray understood him thoroughly. "I've had experience of that kind, too, Stevens. And I'm rapidly gainin' more. Mace'll have to get up early from now on, to catch me asleep."

Late morning saw them drawing near Bluestem Valley once more. It was Ray's turn to point out what he had learned from Euchre and the other outlaws. Indicating a gap in the eastern hills, he showed them where the stock trail leading out from the far-away Culebras turned into the great Outlaw Trail of western Colorado, over which for years stolen stock from as far away as Texas and Montana had passed with impunity.

Reined up on a rocky height, once more they surveyed the vast and desolate emptiness of Bluestem, lonely and peaceful this morning under the sentinel monument of Cloud Peak. Down here the breeze was balmy as Indian summer, but a chill breath now and again blew off the lofty snow fields, presaging the bitter season to come.

Though there appeared little enough to observe, Pat seemed unable to turn away from the majestic scene. He gazed toward the east so long that the others took note of his lingering interest.

"What yuh see, Steven?" Ezra asked gruffly. "Don't tell me I missed somethin' over there—"

Pat shook his head slightly, still at gaze. "Nothin', I guess. The far distance is pretty apt to be hazy at this season . . ." He spoke musingly.

Sloan was using his own keen black eyes to check up on him. "You're noticin' that smoky look, yonder in the hills," he accused. "Spotted that, myself. It *could* be dust. But I reckon it ain't nothin'."

At this juncture Morgan suddenly asserted his own growing confidence in himself. "Maybe it *don't* mean anythin'," he said with stubborn coolness. "Right now it's the only thing in sight worth glancin' at twice—"

His meaning was plain. Pat's deliberate nod was not long delayed. "You're right, Ray. We can't lose by bein' careful . . . We'll jog over that way, just in case. A good healthy surprise is exactly what I'm lookin' for today.''

Dropping down the bald slopes, they struck into the east. Increasingly as they advanced, the land crumpled into rough folds. They followed the low ground, threading the wild brush and working toward the point where Morgan said the cattle trail from the east ran out into the high valley.

The time came when they found themselves in a maze of deep, intersecting washes, the steep cut-banks graphically suggesting the fury of spring and summer storms. In a close group they rode from one sharp turn to the next, watching for any slightest indication of tracks.

None appeared, and not one of the four was prepared for it when, without any warning, an hour later, a sudden dull rumble of hoofs and the restless bellowing of steers broke on their ears, echoing hollowly from no great distance ahead.

Riding in the lead, Pat hauled up sharply. It was uncanny to hear so plainly this swelling clamor and clatter of cattle and at the same time to see absolutely nothing. Then, overhead on their right, a billowing cloud of yellow dust faintly obscured the brilliant noonday sun.

"Wal!" Ezra jerked out harshly, squinting up. "Yuh did see dust, at that. I must be gittin' old!"

The four slid out of the saddle and ran hurriedly to a crevice gashing the side of the wash. Up they clambered, sweating and barking their knees and elbows. At the top Pat clung to a ragged rock pinnacle and gazed over and down. The others were soon at his back, and for long seconds blank surprise held them mute.

Through a wider wash parelleling the one they had been following, moved a strung-out bunch of steers, red-eyed and dust-caked from long travel in this dry country. No attendant rider was in sight at the moment, but Ezra's single eye was clamped on the flanks of those steers with breath-suspended interest.

"What *is* that brand?" he whipped out hoarsely. "Am I goin' dotty—or have yuh been makin' a sale on the side that we ain't heard about, Stevens?"

Pat's own features were rocky and grim as he gazed. Dust and caked dirt made the brands none too easy to decipher, but there could be no mistake. Each of the red-and-white, Herefordstrain steers they were looking at bore the distinctive brand of his own Lazy Mare ranch.

After an interval of petrified attention, Sam Sloan began to laugh. "Interested in rustlin', are yuh? This one's on you, Stevens!" he exclaimed with coarse humor.

For the part, young Morgan had gone white. He read what it meant. "My God, Stevens! The thieves were bold enough to lift this whackin' bunch right under the noses of your own outfit!"

Pat thrust out an admonitory hand, commanding silence. He was gazing hard through the rolling dust. The others saw what he was looking at. A harassed and sweating puncher was forging along in the drag, doing his best to hustle the steers along and not having much luck—and the brand on the dun pony he rode, plainly enough to be seen, was Mace Galloway's jaunty Flagg!

"Wal, Stevens." Ezra's words grated. "Reckon it won't take yuh overlong t' do somethin' about this—"

Pat silently motioned them back, and they slid down to their horses. In a rush, rising to the saddles, they turned back the way they had come, working toward open ground where it would be possible to exert some control over what was going on.

A half hour's cautious scouting apprised them that a good forty or more head comprised the stolen herd and that they were in charge of a trail crew of three men. Although they pushed the steers along briskly, the rustlers appeared in no sense uneasy. Probably they did not dream that an enemy was anywhere within miles of them.

"Yuh lettin' 'em go on, an' see where they go?" Sam demanded.

Pat made his decision quickly. He shook his head. "This seems our chance to grab my stock and head it back," he said tersely. "It may be impossible later to pry it loose. I'll take no unnecessary chances." He had been looking the ground over for some minutes. "They'll break out of the wash a half-mile above here. We'll be ready, an' jump them as they come out." Rapidly he told each of his companions what was expected of him.

"Yuh don't reckon Tigart's crew is around?" persisted Sam.

Pat's smile was mirthless. "Likely they intend to take over at some point. We'll hope to cut in ahead of 'em, Sam. If we don't succeed—" His gesture was expressive.

"If you're figgerin' on takin' that stock in charge, we'll have t' hustle it along," Ezra declared bluntly. "Because sooner or later, Tigart'll be on our tail, any way yuh look at it."

Made tense by the near prospect of gunsmoke, Morgan had little to say, leaving the arrangements to the others. But that he was ready for action was plain fomr his flashing keen face. It was inexperience, and not unwillingness, that drew his nerves taut. Pat saw as much, and he nodded approvingly.

Under the latter's direction they took up their stations in dense brush surrounding the little flat to which the rustled steers must presently come. A faint rumble, and the golden dust haze rising in the air, advertised their approach. Soon the point appeared, a man riding in the lead whom they recognized as having seen recently in Dutch Springs. He was a Flagg hand. Pat waited. The Lazy Mare steers strung out on the flat. A second rustler appeared, hazing the cows along.

Stevens rode out into the path of the lead man and halted his horse with an iron hand. The fellow saw him. He tightened up, sweeping a slitted gaze about. Sight of Morgan and the grizzled partners stayed his hand momentarily.

"Where you goin' with that stock?" Pat rapped out at him sharply.

"Stevens, ain't it?" The man's watchful grin was flat. "All I can say is, I'm under orders. This stuff must've been bought off yore spread while yuh was away—"

As casual as they seemed, the words cam quick and curt. Clearly the outlaw was bracing himself for anything that might come. Bare-faced as his claim was, he did not appear to expect it to be accepted at face value. Nor did Pat disappoint him.

"We'll say yuh won't be goin' any farther, anyway, till I've looked into it," he announced flatly. "First I want to see a bill of sale. Who's in charge here—you?"

Seeing himself cornered, the man got tough. "Yuh won't see nothin' but dust, hombre," he rasped. "Out of our way—" And he came straight at Pat as if intent on riding him down.

Pat made no move to draw aside. His gun crashed, and a slug sang over the fellow's head. Ducking, the rustler whirled his horse and whipped his own gun out. His bullet creased Pat's hatbrim. He never found time for a second shot. Uttering an exclamation, Pat threw down on him with smooth certainty.

Striking the rustler in the shoulder, the slug tore him out of the saddle and slammed him to the ground, where he lay writhing.

Meanwhile, Pat's companions had rushed headlong toward the other rustlers. Seeing themselves unwarningly attacked, the latter threw a couple of wild shots and incontinently fled. Having raced for the protection of the brush, they hauled up long enough to limber a carbine which one of them carried in a saddle boot. With the longer range at his command, the marksman might speedily have evened the odds had his nerve held. But Morgan took matters in hand by boldly charging his position, regardless of whistling slugs which droned close, his own six-gun spitting.

The rattled outlaw fired a last despairing shot, which flew wild, and plunged away, the carbine tumbling out of his nerveless grasp. Ezra methodically recovered it.

"Ray! Come back!" Pat called before the young fellow could pursue his quarry farther. Morgan turned back reluctantly, his face set.

"Atta boy, Morgie!" Sam approved jovially. "Yuh sure fogged that blackleg!"

But Ray's blood was up. "A little more and I'd've got him, too," he rapped out. "We should've knocked off all three of these birds, Stevens! It'd been safest!"

Pat knew he was right, but it had never been his policy to shed blood where it could be avoided. "We've got the steers," he pointed out practically. "Thing to do now is to head 'em the right way and give 'em a shove."

They let the stock water at the nearby creek and, once assured they were not in distress, headed them back over the mountains. Ezra was detailed to keep a watch to the rear. Armed with the carbine he had claimed, he hung back to cover their activities.

It was rough work trying to hurry the travel-worn stock

along. At best Pat knew they would run a few pounds off, and he could not avoid asking himself how Johnson, his shrewd and experienced foreman, had been hoodwinked to this extent.

Early afternoon saw them working up out of the washes at last. An hour later they entered the pines. Here the steeper going slowed them down, but at least the worst of the dust had been left behind. Again and again Pat turned to gaze back. It did not seem likely that pursuit would be on their trail for a number of hours—perhaps not before tomorrow—but one never knew.

He was not surprised, as the shadows began to lengthen under the gnarled pines, to spy Ezra, whom he had not seen for an hour, come pelting up the trail. Pat hauled his horse about and waited. The lanky one soon approached, his bronc in a fine lather.

"Only one thing that would make you hurry that way," he threw at him alertly.

Ezra jerked his head in a nod. "They're after us, Pat! Must be six or eight of 'em, too! I waited long 'nough t' make sure."

"It's Tigart's outfit, of course?"

"Couldn't be no other. I seen 'em stop by that hombre yuh downed, an' they was wavin' their arms an' pointin'. This way," Ez added grimly. "After a few minutes they picked up an' headed out."

Pat digested the intelligence swifty. "There's no chance to cache the stock around here—quick enough to throw 'em off. But we can maybe get 'em shoved through yonder gap. And then it's up to you with that gun, Ez."

The redhead helped them hustle the steers along toward the hills. In a matter of minutes the pursuing outlaws became visible. But the notch in the hills was not far now. Pat could only hope the barrier was impregnable except at that point.

The lead steers lumbered through the rocky gap, their bellows echoing under the dusty pines. Ezra leveled the carbine down the trail and fired. Pat did not even pause to glance back, seeing that the herd drove on through. He and Sam hazed the last stragglers up the stony slope, and they clattered through the notch.

"Keep 'em movin', now!" Ezra called out as he climbed a

great rock beside the trail, directly in the throat of the gap. "I'll give yuh mebbe an hour! Dunno how much longer I kin hold them coyotes off!"

The spang of the saddle gun put a period to his words, and for a long time afterward the others heard the ominous sounds of battle raging in the pass, without any slightest inkling to tell them how it was going.

13.

LEFT ALONE, SPRAWLED OUT atop the high rock in the pine-choked pass, his horse nearby, Ezra studied the back trail with a narrow interest. Throwing a warning shot at the three pounding pursuers visible far below, he wondered what had become of their companions; for on first sighting them he had, as he had told Pat, counted a certain half-dozen and probably not less than seven or eight.

Ezra was himself too good a strategist to miss the strong likelihood that the remainder of Tigart's Flagg warriors were circling his position, with the intent to close in on him from above. To make matters worse, though the carbine he wielded was equipped to accommodate .45-caliber six-gun cartridges, once he had exhausted its original load, it would assuredly be no match for rifle fire from the craggy heights overhead.

Made of stern stuff, the lanky redhead stuck firmly to his post while such thoughts as these flitted through his mind. He succeeded in forcing the trio down there off the trail, one of them with a crippled bronc. They took to cover, but did not give up their frontal attack. Slugs screamed off the front of the rock from their position amongst the ragged pines. They were working forward steadily.

Ezra kept them from taking any wild chances, consequently slowing their advances. The moments dragged. But he knew how time telescoped in such a situation. He would have given much to know how far along the Lazy Mare steers really were by now. Hope of saving them from pursuit by a strong force seemed dubious at best.

He had been firing quickly at the agitated brush a hundred yards down the trail and was levering a fresh shell into the

chamber when a sudden jarring smack on the rough rock near
his hand changed abruptly to a whining scream. Dust, stinging his gaunt cheek, did not prevent his quick look at the
spot. A leaden smear met his eye where a ball, narrowly
missing him, had ricocheted off. Even as he glanced that
way, petrified, Ezra knew the shot could not possibly have
come from down the trail. There was only one other possible
explanation. Already the enveloping movement by the circling outlaws was closing in on him.

He sprang up with a bellow of furious disgust, just as
second slug whined off the spot where he had been lying. He
leapt to the ground with a jarring plunge and flung himself on
his pony, yanking its head around savagely. The air all about
him droned now with bullets like bees. Somehow he escaped
being hit. The astonished horse, under the persuasion of heels
ramming into its flanks, burst running down the trail in the
wake of the steers.

"It's up t' Stevens now," grated Ezra, hugging the saddle
as his racing mount flashed over the rocks underfoot. "I give
'im all the time I could squeeze out—an' dang unlikely it'll
do any good!"

Yells and a fresh outburst of wild shooting from the rear
advertised a close pursuit. So speedily had it come about, the
outlaws rendering his position untenable in so competent a
style, that he had no real hope of Stevens's ability to whisk
the recovered steers out of danger before Tigart's wolves
overtook them. Despite a good try, it was simply one of the
breaks of a very rough game.

Ez no longer bothered to watch behind him, but made the
best of his flight, with a shrewd eye for the first faint possibility of a fresh ambush. Delaying the outlaws further, if that
were humanly possible, would yet enable him to afford Pat
and the others more time with the slow-moving cattle.

So flinty was the faint trail he followed that little or no sign
of the passage of stock could be detected, but the way seemed
plain enough. Ezra stuck to the course he would himself have
pursued with running cattle, expecting every few moments to
overhaul the lagging herd.

But the laboring horse thrust space behind, and still the
steers failed to appear. The big fellow grew uneasy. Already
he had covered a mile or more since leaving the pass. "Hang

that Stevens!'' he burst out in exasperation. ''His steers couldn't've got this far, without flyin'!''

A spent rifle slug, wailing off a lightning-blasted pine stub beside the trail, dissuaded him from pausing long enough to con his doubts. He fired backward once, then drilled on down the empty trail. Twenty minutes later, pursuit appeared to have been shaken off effectually; and still Ezra had failed to overtake the elusive stock. Conviction assailed him as he sat, hauled up on a lonely pine ridge in deep, wind-soughing silence.

''Stevens played it cute,'' he muttered. ''He pulled off the trail while I tolled them owlhoots on past. He's holed up some'eres, safe as a church—if they ain't been smart 'nough t' smell him out. There can't be no other answer . . . Danged if that boy ain't mighty hard t' beat, at that!''

He delayed for an hour, lingering off the trail and watching hawklike, and at the end of that time, nothing whatever having developed, he decided that further action would be in order. Once more he turned back, advancing slowly and quietly through cover a dozen yards away from the trail, lest an outlaw bushwhack attempt awaited.

Evening birds sang and whistled in the pines, and by degrees the light faded. At last only the west bore a streak of dying mauve light Still he had not succeeded in discovering any signs of life. Turning his back to the trail, Ezra sought water and a comfortable spot, which he found under a rocky overhang; and taking up a practical notch in his belt, he settled himself to wait. Only the hoot of fugitive owls and a far-off wailing of coyotes on the hills disturbed his rest.

He awoke, startled, in the gray of dawn, to an echoing clatter of hoofs and snapping of brush below on the trail. Punctuated by a cheerful lowing of steers and the occasional yip of a rider, the sounds were self-explanatory. Ez sprang out of his covert with a grunt of approval. It was a matter of seconds for him to toss on this saddle and cinch up, and a few minutes later he was riding out onto the trail and falling into line beside the lumbering cattle as casually as though he had never been separated from the herd.

Ray Morgan was the first to spot his lanky figure through the growing gray light. ''Hey-y!'' he called excitedly. ''There yuh are! I was afraid yuh'd got snowed under by them gunslingers, Ezra—''

The one-eyed man gave him a half-attentive glance, growling contemptuously. ''Any time them stumble bums knock me off, I'll let yuh know beforehand!'' was all he said.

Ray could not help grinning at his gruffness. Pat jogged up a minute later. ''Good work, Ezra,'' he approved quietly. ''Yuh gave us the extra minutes we needed back there. I didn't have a chance to tip yuh off to my plans, but we couldn't have tricked Tigart's crowd more neatly. I won't swear we're done with 'em, but it's my guess they'll spend the day beatin' the woods a few miles back. We'll take advantage of the opportunity to shove along.''

''I figured yore game, soon as I didn't come up with yuh on the trail,'' Ez nodded. ''Yuh must've run onto a fine spot t' hide these beeves. *I* never noticed where yuh turned off—not that I was lookin' very hard.''

Pat's chuckle was quiet. ''We managed all right,'' was his sole response.

They saw nothing further of the outlaws on that day. Nor, although Ezra and Sam rode on ahead of reconnoiter Badger Pass, did anything occur to delay them at that precarious spot. On the little herd traveled, eating up the miles steadily; and though this was largely outlaw territory through which they were passing, Pat concluded that sheer audacity would see them safely through to Powder Valley.

He was right. On the Ute Gap range, a pertinacious crew of five men brazenly proposed taking the steers off their hands at a preposterous price; but these men obviously had no connection whatever with Mace Galloway's outfit, and Pat succeeded in short order in convincing them that he found no interest in a swindling deal. In the face of a too evenly matched fight, the long riders backed down, and they were allowed to push on unmolested.

On the following morning, snow all but blocked their passage on the high trail through the Culebras. It swirled in a gale round the peaks, and the pine woods rapidly filled with fine sifting flakes. Somehow they persuaded the weary steers to face the last open slopes. Afternoon saw them dropping down out of the storm into balmy, sun-drenched weather, one of the startling contrasts for which Colorado was notorious in winter.

Pat and the partners cheered perceptibly. It was clear to the former, however, that young Morgan's uneasiness only increased as they reached the lower levels. At last he spoke up.

"What's bothering yuh, Red?" he asked. "Yuh got somethin' or other on your mind."

Ray hesitated before replying. "I've got no notion of quittin' yuh, Stevens," he blurted out. "But I can't wait to get over to my place—"

Pat's gray eyes appraised him with ready understanding. "I get it, boy." He smiled. "You've simply got to find out how Candace has been doin' over there—and in your place, I'd feel the same way."

"What are yuh waitin' for, then, Morgan?" Sam Sloan struck in, riding close. "Git on yer way! We kin shove this handful o' cows down onto Lazy Mare range easy enough. An' we'll be seein' yuh. Before long, too."

It was his offhand assurance that they did not intend to wash their hands of either the young fellow himself or such troubles as he might still find himself possessed of, and Ray shot him a grateful glance.

"Thanks, boys," he got out with difficulty. "Reckon I owe yuh a heap already. Maybe I can pay it back someday."

"We'll take the wish for the deed," Sam growled. "It ain't ever'body, nowdays, that so much as bothers t' say thanks!"

Ray did not wait for more, but turned his horse away and headed it directly toward the Star Cross. Inarticulate as Morgan was by nature, he felt the strong drag of a lodestone in the prospect of riding back onto the only property he had ever owned. That such a fine girl as Candace awaited him there added its irresistible tug to his heart. He had learned to feel more warmly about her than he was ready to admit as yet, even to himself.

But when he rode into the Star Cross yard half an hour later, Ray's heart unaccountably sank. No pony stamped about his corral or stood waiting at the kitchen door. There was in point of fact no slightest appearance of anyone's having been there for days. Had he really expected as much? Striving to fight off leaden disappointment, he bethought himself of China Springs. Of course! There, on his hard-bought winter range where his cattle were, if anywhere, he might most reasonably expect to find the girl. But at this hour? Once more it approached dwindling twilight, with night in the offing.

Kicking his bronc that way, Ray knew only that he wanted to see Candace again, and at once, more than he had ever wanted anything in his life.

It was still faintly light when he burst into the lush meadowland surrounding the springs, only to haul up in fresh dismay. A few Star Cross steers lingered there, at graze, but the bulk of his little herd had drifted off and were gone from sight. Clearly, if anyone had been riding herd on them recently, it had not been on this day.

What inference might be drawn from this, Morgan was at a loss to decide. Had Candace given up her care of his precarious interests—perhaps under pressure of force? It would be like old Zep Cowan to drag the girl off home, spouting wrath and resentment, regardless of what might happen to Ray's unguarded stock.

Both Morgan and Candace had reached the age of mature responsibility. Sitting his horse rocklike in the deepening shades of dusk, the young fellow thought he could be pretty sure of what had taken place. With equal certainty, he had no intention of allowing matters to rest in this posture.

"I'll barge over to the Bull's Head now, make my play—and be damned to old Cowan," he reflected bleakly. "Either he's got to get used to me, or we'll break each other's necks. So what's holdin' me back?"

He would have hesitated to put a name to his reason for widely avoiding Dutch Springs on his way to Cowan's ranch, wary as he yet was of Sheriff Lawlor. But in any event the night effectually concealed him. After striking the Hopewell Junction road, he was soon at the turnoff leading to Candace's home.

Lights were burning in the modest ranch house, and stock could be heard moving about the barn and the tangle of pole corrals beyond. Ray hoped the girls father might be busy at work there, safely out of the way. But, scorning either spying or indirection, he rode boldly up to the door.

His knock brought a masculine bellow from within, and the

door swung back. Light from the kitchen lamp flashed side-wise on old Zep's ruddy face.

"Yeh—" he called, peering out into the darkness. "Who is it?"

The young fellow braced himself, "Mr. Cowan, it's Ray Morgan," he spoke up stoutly. "I've come to see—Candace, please."

"What!" Cowan literally exploded in heady wrath. "Of all the unmitigated gall! Wal, Morgan—yuh can't see my girl, an' yuh won't see her! What's more, yuh'll git off my ranch in a hurry, before I take a shotgun to yuh!"

He could not have made his position plainer. Ray took a step back, flushing, but held his ground. "If Candace tells me herself she don't want to see me, I'll go," he exclaimed. "Are yuh givin' her that chance, Cowan?"

"No!" Old Zep hurled the word at him, in freezing denial and rejection. "She don't want nothin' t' do with you! *I* say so, an' that's aplenty!"

"But, look here, Cowan—" Ray began in husky appeal.

The scarlet-faced rancher cut him off with a roar. "Myra!" he bawled, beside himself with fury. "Where's my Greener? Bring it here. Quick!"

Morgan had seen Candace's mother hovering nervously behind her agitated husband, but there was no evidence of the girl's presence. Tumbling hastily into the saddle, Ray pulled away before matters got altogether out of hand.

"Damn him!" he ejaculated under his breath as he rode away. "Reckon he knows I can't put the slug on Candace's dad, no matter how I feel." Yet the apparent disappearance of the girl troubled him deeply. "Hang it all! I wonder what Stevens'll make of this crazy deal?"

It was a late hour when he rode up to the darkened Lazy Mare ranch house that night, but Crusty Hodge eventually answered his banging summons.

"Who is that—young Morgan?" Pat's voice sounded from somewhere within as the door swung back. "Tell him to come in, Crusty."

Ray found the Lazy Mare owner in bed, the blankets pulled to his chin. Shading his face from the light of a lantern with his palm, Pat listened to the other's story. That he was displeased was clear from his frown at the end.

"There can't much be done tonight," he said at length. "Put up your pony, Morgan, and roll into a bunk here. I'll ride into town in the mornin' and ask around. Yuh might be able to meet Candace there, if she knows she can expect yuh."

It was so arranged, after some further discussion. Ray got but little sleep, however, for he tossed restlessly the remainder of that night. Yet he possessed himself with such patience as he could muster while Stevens saddled up the following morning and jogged away toward Dutch Springs. He was back at the end of a long two hours, shaking his head darkly as he met Ray's anxious look.

"She ain't been seen in town for several days, Red," he announced bluntly. "It looks bad. But maybe the answer's simple enough. Old Cowan's certainly on the warpath, and Candace can hardly be blamed for layin' low—"

Ray bounced off the porch step to stride back and forth. He poured out his fears and his threats toward Cowan, releasing his pent feelings. Pat waited till he had calmed down somewhat.

"Get your horse, boy," he urged then. "We'll go back to the Star Cross, if yuh want, and try to take this business apart. You *could've* missed something, yuh know."

But when they rode into Morgan's yard at midmorning, the little ranch lay as empty and enigmatic as before. Nothing at the barn gave any clue to recent activity there, the dust in the corral was a blank, and they were moving about through the musty, shut-in house when gruff voices and a faint thud of hooves outside drew their attention.

"Somebody's out there," exclaimed Ray, with sudden hope. "It's either Sam and Ez, or else—"

He rushed to the door, then halted in the opening as abruptly as if suddenly turned to stone. Over his shoulder, Pat was only faintly surprised to glimpse Candace's peppery father, sitting his saddle as obdurate as a stump and glowering hotly at Morgan.

"There he is, Lawlor!" Cowan rumbled to the keen-eyed man at his side. "Yuh may claim he ain't nowhere in the county, but I don't have no particular trouble in stumblin' over him! Better take him in charge, b'fore he sneaks away again!"

Disdaining to avoid this open challenge, Ray stepped out

into the yard and shouldered up to the Sheriff, who coolly dismounted to meet him. Their eyes met squarely. There was a jangle of metal, and in a twinkling Jess had snapped one of the handcuffs on the young fellow's wrist.

"Well, of all the high-handed operations! . . . What's the particular meanin' of this business, Lawlor?" rasped Ray, in tense amazement.

"Cowan here accuses yuh of abductin' his girl," the lawman dropped briefly, through thin lips. "Mebby yuh got an alibi, Morgan—but this time you're comin' along till it's all straightened out!"

Ray whirled to direct a blind appeal toward Pat, who was taking it all in without change of expression. Weighing the matter calmly, Pat took his time, but in the end he shook his head decidedly.

"Something's dead wrong here," he said flatly. "But we certainly can't iron it out by flyin' off the handle . . . Better go along with 'em, Morgan, till I've had my own chance to look into this."

Ray was so stunned by this sudden mischance, dashing a hand blindly across his brows, that his tone was muffled. "I can only hope you're not givin' me a load of double talk, Stevens," he exclaimed. "If it'd been yore intention from the start to bring me back and turn me over to the law, yuh couldn't have arranged it better."

"If yuh look at it that way." Pat's answer was colorless, betraying by no word or sign the sting he found in the groundless accusation. "Time alone'll prove whether you're right or not. So why should I argue?"

Mounting his horse with mechanical awkwardness, and avoiding the eyes of these men, Morgan allowed himself to be led off toward the jail.

14.

As SAM SLOAN STEPPED jauntily out of the Bar ES ranch house into bright morning sunlight, his rakish hat lifted off his head apparently of it own volition and sailed majestically off to land ten feet away in the dust. He made an ineffectual grab at it, crouched suddenly as the significance of the strange occurrence belatedly dawned on him, and then sprang back inside the door.

Wiping his mouth on a rumpled sleeve, having just finished his morning coffee, Ezra turned to stare at his partner, his single eye piercing as he caught the faint crack of a distant rifle.

"What in thunder was that?" he rasped alertly.

Meeting his glance, Sam gestured outside significantly. "Visitors," was his terse response. "Somebody who took me for you, I wouldn't wonder. Anyway, he don't like us."

Ezra rolled it over for ten seconds, growling in this throat, "Good cripes! That can't be Tigart, payin' his compliments already—"

Grabbing up an old campaign hat of his own, Ezra moved over to a door opposite the one from which Sloan had stepped and cautiously eased its brim round the sill, like a man peeping. Promptly there came a dull thud as a slug lodged in the logs of which the structure was composed, not far from his hand.

Ez straightened, scratching his grizzled thatch. "Dang poor shot," he grumbled. "Missin' at four or five hundred yards like that—"

His satire was meant to convey precisely the opposite

112

meaning; for few men, even in a land where all men handled guns more or less familiarly, could have done as well. Sam got the point without any trouble.

"He didn't miss mine," he grumbled grimly. "It's out there on the ground with a hole in it yuh could put yore fist through." A thoughtful expression overspread his pudgy features, causing the bushy black brows to twitch. "Ez, supposin' that t' be part of Galloway's tough crowd—what would them hombres want of us?"

"Why, they—" Ezra broke off, arrested. His look was suddenly that of an aroused eagle. "Shucks! They wouldn't have the gall t' make a play for our hosses!" he said explosively.

"Mebby not." Sam was curt. "But I wouldn't bet on it, an' expect t' collect."

Ezra knew he was right. It was strictly in line with what had already been happening for the Flagg outfit to show its hand sooner or later in brazen boldness. Mace Galloway had been growing in power of late. He was in solid with Sheriff Lawlor as one of the more important business men of the valley. Doubtless Mace felt confident of his ability to divert any serious threat to the lawless gang he headed, no matter how raw their depredations.

Ezra was just now painfully conscious of the score or more of unusually fine roan horses being held in the south pasture. An outlaw crew on the make might well be calculated to covet such a haul. There was little doubt in the mind of either partner that this was the true object behind the surprise morning attack.

Rifle in hand, Sam was peering out through the chinks between the logs on the west side of the cabin. "Somebody out there on the slope," he muttered. "Can't make out much—"

His rifle crashed a moment later. Ezra had taken down his own and was doing his best to locate a target. He moved out into a lean-to shed adjoining the ranch house and was making for the open side when a spent slug rattled amongst the loose kindling piled at his side. Ezra started and swore.

Withdrawing to the door, he called over this shoulder. "Watch it, runt! They're on two sides of us."

The fact eliminated any possibility of chance in the manner of this systematic siege. Both read the determined design behind the attack. They were to be pinned here inside the ranch house for as long as it suited the outlaws—or to be wiped out.

"They're closin' in," Sam announced, levering a cartridge into the firing chamber. "They won't have no particular luck, tryin' t' take us by storm."

Despite the cottonwoods shading the yard and giving the place a pastoral air, the ranch house had been built by original plan in the center of an open flat, which rendered close approach virtually impossible without observation. But in the present case, defense was not their sole concern.

"Better make our play while there's time," remarked Sam uneasily. "Is there any chance of smokin' 'em once we get horseflesh under us?"

"Wal, I've counted five o' them buzzards," rejoined Ez dryly. "An' more seem t' be showin' up. I dunno how many *you* feel like takin' on—"

"We'll just say they take the pot." Sam grinned. "It's a heap easier that way."

Despite his levity, it was with the greatest reluctance that Sloan faced the necessity of abandoning the ranch, even should they by enabled thus to slip away unscathed. But he had long since learned to accept an unescapable fact as such, and he did not vacillate now.

"What yuh aimin' t' try?" he demanded briefly.

Ezra shrugged. "Wall, if we kin gather them broncs, an' fog 'em out of here, that'll be somethin'."

Sam made no comment, ready as he was to try any desperate expedient. Still he was somewhat flabbergasted by these rapid-fire events. "We've had stock run off at night, an' a cute trick or two pulled on us," he groused. "This is the first time I ever knowed a bunch o' crooks t' come ridin' right in after our broncs—an' mighty confident of gittin' 'em!"

"They may git 'em yet, if yuh don't git a hump on yuh," his lanky companion retorted unfeelingly.

Sam snorted, "Lead off, long legs," he snapped. "I'll run fast as I can, an' then start rollin'!"

Having backed away from the door, Winchester in hand,

Ezra started fast and was running as tight as he could go by the time he burst through the door. Sam followed suit. So close was the watch kept on the house as the besiegers closed in that they had not covered more than a dozen yards before dust puffed up about their flying feet. The crack of rifles could be heard distinctly now, but the marksmen were yet too far away to have any luck in firing at their running figures.

Reaching a corral, Ezra kicked the bars flying, darted inside, and swarmed onto the back of a surprised horse before it had guessed what to expect. The animal reared and came down pounding. Ez took time, mounted bareback as he was, to crowd several other ponies into a corner, where Sam, despite his shorter legs, had no great difficulty in procuring a mount.

"Haze 'em down to the pasture," called Ezra, wincing as rifle slugs buzzed by his head in invisible menace. The outlaws had quickly seen what was afoot and were doing their best to break it up.

Shoving the half-dozen saddle horses before them, the partners went clattering down the lane. Their roan herd could be seen, scattered about the wide pasture, pointed ears pricked up and heads turned toward them as the spirited animals sensed swift action.

"Work toward the gate," Sam yelled, sweeping wide on his pony. "We'll be comin' fast in a couple o' minutes!"

He was as good as his word. Ezra barely had time to swing the pasture gate back when with a thunder of pounding hooves, the roans swept forward, close bunched, manes tossing and tails flying like banners.

Out onto the open range they flashed, traveling at express-train speed. Sam and Ezra clung close to their flanks, knowing full well that the thieves would be likely to think twice before firing directly at these magnificent brutes, regardless of the provocation.

Through the dust of their swift passage, Ez was using his single eye to good advantage. It did not take him long to find the weak spot in the cordon being drawn about them.

"Swing 'em north," he bawled.

It was not easy, for the roans were taking the bit in their

teeth at a speed that none but their own breed could have matched. Lead sang over their heads as the raiders raced out to head them off. Sam spied six or seven renegades breaking into the open at alarmingly close range, all bent on turning the racing herd. But the animals were not to be turned this time.

"Right on through!" Sam yelped, with a shrill cowboy cry. His own gun was spitting, and one of the racing outlaws tumbled from his mount with a broken shoulder. It angered the others. Making a determined bid to block off the flight of the coveted horses, they all but allowed themselves to be run down. Still it was without effect. Three minutes later, and the Bar ES roans were through their barricade and running free, neither Ezra nor Sam having sustained a scratch.

"They'll be floggin' after us, Ez, nervy as they are," Sam warned, looking back through the boiling dust.

"Is that supposed t' be news?" the lanky man barked. "We're gittin' out fast as we kin. It won't be healthy for 'em t' crowd us too close, an' I reckon they've caught on!"

Shoving the roans along, by common consent they struck across the hills toward Pat Stevens's Lazy Mare range. Once beyond the restraint of fences, the mettlesome animals clattered through the brush at a great rate.

Ezra dropped back once to reconnoiter the rear. Sam heard the crack of his rifle. Five minutes later the big tracker caught up once more.

"They still comin'?" Sam asked.

"Checkin' on where we're headin' for, anyway," returned Ezra. "I slowed 'em up a bit. But we can't hope t' shake 'em off."

Half an hour later, skimming across the slopes, they came in sight of the Lazy Mare headquarters. They drove straight toward the ranch, and the herd pounded into the yard in a swirl of dust.

Pat came hurrying out of a storage shed where he had been rummaging, attracted by the sudden racket. He flashed a grin at the dirt-grimed partners, at the same time admiring the frisky roans.

"Great bunch of stock, boys" he called. "But I could've said as much over at your place, and saved yuh trouble—"

The smile faded from his jaws as Ez gruffly acquainted him with what had occurred this morning. Reading its significance in a flash, he made an expressive gesture, indicative of impatience, resignation and hardening resolve.

"It's come sooner than I expected," he remarked briefly. "The chances are good that I'll feel the pinch, too . . . Give me two minutes to get up a bronc, boys. We can at least tuck the roans away in a safe place."

Within less than the time mentioned, he jogged out of the corral astride a trim buckskin pony. "Unlimber your shotgun, Crusty, and keep a watch around the place," he called out to Hodge, who wa gaping at them from the porch.

The old rawhide waved in understanding, fierce alertness in his manner. The three horsemen started the Bar ES horses out of the yard. In a moment they were on the move again at a fast clip.

"Where to?" Ezra demanded, looing across the bobbing backs at Pat.

"Make for the creek," was the answer. "We'll turn east there and break trail, just in case—then we'll head for Pinnacle Rocks."

Reaching the shallow stream presently, they turned the horses up its course and followed it for a half-mile before Pat indicated a place where they could turn out onto rocky ground. By a devious course, leaving a minimum of signs behind them, they found themselves at the Pinnacles.

Ragged lava spires and jumbles of rock rose out of the center of a little valley where plentiful feed would virtually insure against the straying of stock, even without a guard being kept. Here the roans were allowed to slow and spread, and they presently fell to grazing.

Ez looked back toward the south, an expression of satisfaction on his gaunt face. "Reckon that'll hold 'em awhile," he growled. "Dunno but it'd fool *me* t' foller our sign here, if I didn't know."

"You'll be all right here," Pat agreed. "But I don't like this business a bit, with Galloway tearin' loose all over the place. Jess Lawlor ought to be notified at once—not that he'll believe the evidence of his eyes. We'll just have to rub his nose in the facts till he begins to see reason."

"I'll ride t' town right off, an' get either Jess or Rufe Dade on the job," Sam proposed.

"That's a good idea." Pat paused reflectively. "I'll stick around with Ez for a while, just to be on the safe side—but we've always got Johnson and the rest of my crew to depend on, in a pinch."

It was so arranged, Sloan pulling away a few minutes later and striking a safely roundabout course through the hills toward town. Pat and Ezra kept a watch from high ground; and though they saw riders several miles away, once or twice during the afternoon, no one came to the Pinnacles. Early dusk found the two friends seated at the base of the rocks, talking the situation over.

"No tellin' what luck Sam may have had," Pat was saying, "But it's unlikely now that Lawlor or Dade'll show up here before mornin'."

"I'll keep a watch." Ezra nodded. "Sam might be back with some news—"

"And if he isn't," Pat caught him up, "yuh won't eat unless we do somethin' about it. Why not ride in to the ranch with me tonight?"

"No, I'll stay here."

Though Pat reasoned with him, Ezra was adamant, and it was finally decided that he should ride the mile or two to Pat's Box Springs line camp, where he could pick up something to eat from the stock of supplies kept there, while Pat awaited his return. The big fellow rode away on this errand. He was back about dark, and after a few minutes' further talk, Pat set out alone for his ranch, more than a little curious to know whether the Flagg raiders had had the effrontery to show up there.

The faint possibility that even now they might still be lingering about caused him to approach the ranch house an hour later with considerable care. Neither seeing nor hearing anything out of the ordinary, he turned his horse quietly into a corral and made for the house. A faint light in the kitchen announced that Crusty Hodge was there waiting. Verifying the fact by means of a glance through the window, Pat started for the door.

Just as he swung the door back to enter, one of its upper

panels gave forth a loud and startling thump not unlike the thud of a drum, and out of the corner of his eye he saw flying splinters.

Pat leapt through, dodging aside in the same motion and slamming the door shut in a hurry. Old Crusty stood in the middle of the floor staring at the table, where the unheralded slug had capsized a pan, ruining it in the process.

"What in tarnation—?" he snarled in shrill wrath.

"They're on our backs," exclaimed Pat warningly. "Get out of that light, Crusty . . . You haven't seen or heard anythin' till now?"

Hodge's negative was profane. "How in tunket yuh expect me t' see anything in pitch dark—!" he began. A second slug, smashing the window and fluttering past his face, caused him to break off abruptly and dive for shelter behind the stove. "Hang it, Stevens, this is yore fault!" he raged. "Yuh go out of yore way t' make enemies o' these birds—an' this is what yuh git for it!"

Pat was well aware of their predicament as still more bullets drove into the house from the cover of darkness outside. Crawling to a gun rack, he lifted down a carbine for himself and another for Crusty. But it was mainly a gesture of preparedness in the event that the outlaws mounted a direct assault, for, as the old man had said, little enough could be seen now. The late moon would not be up for hours, if indeed it showed itself at all on this night.

"Dowse that light," Pat directed, the muttering handyman being closest to it by a number of feet. "Least we can do is to make it as hard as possible for 'em to see what they're shootin' at."

Crusty complied intrepidly. The light blinked out, plunging the entire house in gloom. The shape of its silhouette must have been plain enough to the killers outside, for their balls continued to thud into the clapboard wall, most of them continuing on through and whining about the kitchen in lethal fragments.

"Dang it all, Pat—they'll git us, even here on the floor!" Hodge burst out in fury as a sailing splinter gouged a furrow in his leathery cheek. "Reckon our once chance is t' crawl out the back door an' try t' slip away—"

"No, we won't be driven to that." Pat's tone was sober. "Take it easy, old top. If it gets worse, of course, we'll have to come up with somethin'. But I'm damned if I'll be driven out of my home by those blacklegs, even if they are makin' a sieve of it!"

As the minutes passed and the fire grew hotter if anything, rattling outside in the darkness in a perfect fusillade, it grew apparent to Stevens that the men out there were intent on getting him. Doubtless they were under orders this time to make a job of it, and it looked as though they might succeed.

15.

A RATTLING BURST OF SHOTS raked the kitchen door, the slugs buzzing dangerously about the room. The crash of dishes and clatter of utensils was almost constant. Old Crusty moved about nervously as glancing lead clanged off the stove.

"One o' them bullets'll git us yet, Stevens," he fumed. "I'm either takin' to the cellar, or givin' myself up!"

There was a root cellar under this end of the house. Neither very elaborate nor very deep, it might afford protection of a kind. But Pat was strongly disinclined to retire to it, for one cogent reason.

"If those killers take a notion to fire the house, we'd be roasted like ducks down there," he pointed out calmly. "It ain't beyond 'em, if they figure there's any doubt about our finish."

"Wal, I'm goin' some'eres, an' not wastin' no time about it," Crusty burst out, tense with exasperation.

Pat pondered briefly. The constant rattle of gunfire from the darkness outside did not encourage delay. There were not many safe spots in this one-story frame house at the moment, but he believed he knew of one at least which the marksmen out in the brush had not yet considered. In a corner of the kitchen, a wall ladder led up through a trap door to the raftered roof space above. Although gunmen could rake the roof easily enough with slugs from almost any point in the yard, they must all range upward from the eaves, so that a man stretched out on the rafters up there would be comparatively safe. At least he would have a chance to survive. Pat explained this to Hodge in a guarded undertone.

"We'll try it, anyhow," he said. "Then if they do monkey

around with fire, we can crawl out the little window up there, get on the shed roof, and slide down.''

Crusty was game to try anything that would remove him from this constant threat to life and limb. At a lull in the attack he crawled out from behind the stove, scuttled to the ladder, and hauled himself upward.

''Quiet, now,'' Pat warned, grinning to himself in the darkness at the other's undignified agility. ''Even so much as a tumbled board might give this game away—''

A moment later, assured that Hodge had disappeared through the trap, he followed, swarming quietly upward with equal haste and pulling himself out onto the rafters, where he lay stretched at full length.

''We won't be doin' no shootin' back from up here,'' muttered his companion, although both had prudently retained their firearms.

''Not unless they bust in downstairs to finish us off,'' Pat assented. On the other hand, it suited him that except for a retaliatory shot or two at first, no return firing had been done from the house, useless as it was in this enveloping gloom. By no means sure whether their lethal purpose had been accomplished, the outlaws would inevitably be left uncertain by this ambiguous silence, and consequently much slower to rush the place regardless of their numbers.

That they did not yet believe their task done was attested by the ominous regularity with which slugs continued to rip into the walls below. Scarcely a spot anywhere in the ground floor of the house remained unprobed. The renegades were leaving absolutely nothing to chance. Listening critically to the muted gunfire from outside, Pat judged the gunmen to have completely surrounded the place, in precisely the same manner as Ezra declared had happened at the bar ES.

''Nothing haphazard about this business,'' he reflected grimly. It told him more plainly than words that a shrewd intelligence guided the actions of these men. More certainly than ever he guessed at the identity of that malevolent spirit. Who could it be but the man who had tried determinedly to smash young Ray Morgan? Who but Mace Galloway?

''They're workin' closer, Stevens!'' Crusty muttered in uneasy concern. ''We can't hope t' stick this out all night—''

Pat had long since come to a similar conclusion, but what

Hodge had overlooked was the obvious fact that the noise of any such protracted siege as this was certain to carry a long way. Assuredly someone must hear it.

For another long twenty minutes, during which they deemed their dilemma progressively more critical, there was no apparent sign that anyone had heard the shooting or meant to do anything about it. Then Pat froze, listening alertly. He turned his face blindly toward Crusty's position.

"Hear anythin' different our there?" It was a breathless query.

"What?" growled the old man grumpily.

"Listen close—"

It seemed to Pat that he could detect a sudden scattered increase in the firing outside. A moment later he was sure when an alarmed yell drifted to their ears. Moreover, the slugs had ceased abruptly their endless thudding into the house walls.

Next came the faint clatter of ponies. They swept toward the house, while more than one rattling fusillade broke out in the brush, ominous and sharp. Yells echoed behind the sheds, and one at least sounded mortal. Gradually the shooting drew away and faded over the range. A dead silence enveloped the ranch house, this moment of letdown somehow more sinister than the drumming of gunfire had been.

Old Crusty eased his position on the rafters, striving to force his cracked tones into naturalness. "Somethin's happened," he growled with gusty relief. "Reckon them hombres're busier now'n they was before!"

Pat was already feeling his way toward the trap door, then letting himself down into the darkness below. "I looked for somethin' of the kind to happen," he admitted. "We'll let the boys know we're still in circulation."

Striking a match in the kitchen, he looked in vain for a lamp that still remained in working condition, till he bethought himself of a battered lantern resting on the stairs leading down to the root cellar. It had escaped destruction, and he was lighting it when a man ran up the porch steps to bang on the sagging door.

"Pat!" It was Ezra's voice, strained now with genuine concern. "Are yuh there—?"

Pat laughed as he undid the catch and kicked the door back, its panels in splintered shreds.

"We're here—and still all in one piece, Ez," he answered. "Crusty's got a scratch or two, but that's all."

Stepping in, the one-eyed man glanced about with dropped jaw at the evident destruction here and then looked at Stevens incredulously.

"Yuh mean the two of yuh lived through this?" he exclaimed hoarsely. "Dang good thing it didn't take me no longer t' ride after Johnson an' the boys, an' bring 'em back here!"

"Crusty says amen to that." Pat grinned as the handyman let himself down the ladder, still muttering his lugubrious wrath. "If we hadn't thought of the rafters up there, we might not either one of us be talkin' it over now."

Not yet had Ezra got over his amazement at their good fortune, if such it was. "How in hell did yuh hold 'em off this long?" he rasped.

"Wouldn't say we have much to do with it, except to keep 'em guessing." Pat shrugged. "They seemed to be takin' their time—perhaps with some idea of makin' double sure of a thorough job."

He paused as more men stepped through the door to look around in stolid amazement. Johnson, his foreman, followed by several Lazy Mare punchers, vouchsafed him a brief but steady regard, expressing the same surprise at his survival as Ezra had felt. The grizzled ramrod took his time then to look the place over, missing none of the wreckage.

"Nice mess for a bunch of grown men to leave," he commented briefly. "Who was it?"

Pat waved a hand. "Who'd be this interested in us, besides our friends over on the Flagg range?"

A direct man, Johnson growled in his throat, anger darkening his leathery face. "We'll ride on over there now, if yuh say the word—"

"No," Pat vetoed decidedly. "I'll do somethin' about it, but in my own time . . . Just so we're sure that bunch has been driven off."

"They won't come back," the foreman assured him tersely. "There's one of 'em in the brush that ain't going' nowheres—"

During the next hour, the Lazy Mare hands drifted back as

the scattered pursuit petered out. Crusty managed to scare up an unpunctured pan for coffee, and considerable discussion ensued. Retiring to the bunkhouse, the crew turned in for what remained of the night, Ezra and Pat following suit at the house.

Daylight saw them afoot once more, and none too soon. Soon afterward, Pat saw Sam Sloan jogging into the ranch yard with Sheriff Lawlor in tow. Standing in the door, he waited for them to approach.

Even to Lawlor's eye, the scars of the night's raid were all too plain. Windows were broken out, the clapboard walls splintered and torn. "Wal!" the lawman exclaimed. "Sloan was tellin' me a wild story, Stevens, but I never expected this!" He looked the house over with concern. "Somebody was sure interested in polishin' yuh off. Who was it?" he queried bluntly.

"It was Mace Galloway, Jess," Pat told him flatly.

"Galloway!" It came out in a snort, and the Sheriff's steady regard grew quizzical. "Recognized him in the dark, I reckon." he remarked sarcastically.

"Damn it, Lawlor!" Pat pretended hot impatience. "Come with me." He led the way out into the brush where daylight revealed a man sprawled out, a ragged wound in his throat. "There's one of 'em the boys nailed last night. We left him for you. Take a good look!"

Lawlor did so. It happened to be the puncher who had been in charge of the rustled steers recovered in Bluestem Valley. Jess could not have known that, of course, but he did identify the man quickly enough as a Flagg hand. He listened silently while Pat described the recent raids on his ranch, culminating in the affair across the mountains.

"You've been pointin' a finger at Ray Morgan all this while, for every bit of deviltry that's turned up," Pat concluded sternly. "That's exactly what the real crooks have wanted yuh to think . . . Better wise up, Lawlor, before Galloway makes a monkey out of you!"

Jess's expression was mocking. "Wouldn't that be terrible, now?" he murmured, obviously unready to believe a word Pat said.

The latter would not leave him alone, however. "Well, there's damage to my property here, and mighty heavy at that," he challenged levelly. "Are you aimin' to do anything about it?"

"I'll tote that dead man away," said Jess stolidly. "And I'll promise yuh the same as I did Sloan—I'll look into the matter. If it comes down to ridin' over and throwin' it all in Mace Galloway's teeth, Stevens," he ended bluntly, "the answer is no."

"Dang it, Sheriff," Sam burst out. "Yuh ain't forgettin', are yuh, that it was two Flagg hands who got mixed up in that deal at the post office in Dutch Springs—?"

"Wal, I ain't satisfied in my own mind about that, yet," Lawlor allowed. "But their workin' for Mace don't necessarily mean nothin'—nor this feller either!"

Pat threw his hands up in disgust. "Don't try to tell him his business, Sloan," he said contemptuously. "He don't know what it is himself. But he won't listen to a word about his friend Galloway. That wouldn't be right!"

Right or wrong. Lawlor did not propose to listen any longer to any such sarcasm as this. Leaving them abruptly, he had his solitary look around the ranch and, after borrowing an extra horse, packed the corpse aboard and presently disappeared in the direction of town.

"Big help, he is," Sam remarked, gazing after him.

"Well, I've got an ace of my own left," Pat rejoined briefly. "Lawlor can't complain now if I elect to play it my own way—"

"Huh?" Sam was gruffly curious. "What'll yuh do?"

"I'll ride over to the Flagg this mornin' and tackle Galloway," Pat told him unemotionally. "If Lawlor won't touch it, maybe *I* can slow him up."

"Somethin' t' that." Sam nodded. Without further comment he went for his pony and waited till Pat was ready. They set off across the range, Ezra having already jealously returned to his watch over the Bar ES roans.

Late forenoon saw the pair drawing near the Flagg ranch. At Pat's suggestion, Sam hung back while he rode on to the ranch alone. Galloway's headquarters was a pretentious log structure built on a bench amidst shading pines. Pat rode around the corner of the house and, ignoring a staring Flagg puncher in the yard, shoved his bronc close to the door, then pounded on it without dismounting.

A man inside answered, swift alarm leaping to his raw-boned face as his eye fell on the visitor.

Pat was short with him. "Get Galloway out here."

The man fell back. A moment later, Mace Galloway himself shouldered to the door. His cheeks suddenly going dusky, eyes like gray ice, he regarded Pat closely.

"Why—howdy, Stevens! I must say I'm a little surprised to see yuh over here. Thought yuh was busy with round-up . . . What's yore errand?"

His crude attempt at heartiness fell flat. Pat eyed him inscrutably, without change of expression.

"We'll skip the formalities, Galloway," he advised. "I think we understand each other pretty well . . . It so happens, after a little scoutin' around, that I've got the deadwood on yuh."

Mace went violently red, thus betraying his knowledge of guilt. His expression of amazement, promptly assumed, was obviously forced. "That's strange talk, Stevens," he rolled out with an effort at indignation. "I got no slightest idea what you're drivin' at—"

Pat's nod was curt. "I can understand it wouldn't occur to you that I'm wise to your activities in—Bluestem Valley, let's say—not to mention the trail between here and there!"

"Bluestem?" Galloway's face was perfectly blank. "Where's that?"

Pat chuckled mirthlessly. If he had hoped to force some admission from this ice-blooded man, he was failing. "Any-how, I blocked yuh there. You'll learn, Galloway—if yuh haven't heard. I think yuh have." His manner hardened. "You're hot because I brought Morgan back. But that isn't all I've been up to lately." He delayed to give his next words full effect. "Call off your dogs, Mace—or I'll pull the plug."

Galloway was glaring at Stevens now with undisguised hatred. "That sounds like a threat," he said slowly and sourly. "I still don't know what you're gettin' at, Stevens. But I don't expect to let it worry me." His flat defiance was flinty. "Go ahead! Do yore worst, and I'll undertake to tough it out."

Pat had not expected any other answer. He pulled his horse around, then paused. "Fair enough—since you're the kind that has to be shown. But understand this, Mace." His words dropped now like stones. "One more stab at those Bar ES horses, or my steers either, and I'll be over here again—and bring my friends with me."

Galloway laughed at him, his harshness belying any intent of mirth. "On yore way, Stevens. And count yoreself lucky you're able to make it!" It was his last word.

Rejoining Sam without haste, Pat shook his head at the other's eager questions. "I didn't have much luck, Sam, except that Galloway's fully warned of what to expect," he said. "I didn't leave any doubt in his mind about that."

"So what now?" the squat man asked.

"I keep thinkin' of young Morgan," Pat confessed. "With him in jail, and Candace droppin' out of sight, it's enough to worry anybody what's happenin' over at his place. Candace may have gone to work over there again . . . We'll ride over and look around the Star Cross."

It was not far to Morgan's little ranch from the Flagg range, and they were soon looking down into the hollow in which Ray's modest home was situated. No one at all appeared to be about just then.

"Yuh reckon Galloway may take another crack at Morgan while he's put outa the way?" Sam inquired as they rode down there.

Pat shrugged. "He'll lash out in any direction he many happen to think of—particularly if he gets leery. In Morgan's boots, I'd be mighty wary of that wolf—" He broke off and hauled in with a jerk at they started to enter the Star Cross yard, his staring gaze fastened on a tumbled bundle of clothing lying in the dirt not ten feet from Morgan's door. All too manifestly, it was a lifeless body. "What was I just sayin'?" His voice grated harshly. "Somebody's been knocked off—"

"Yes—an' it's a girl!" Sam's voice rose in a wrathy yelp, as he shoved his horse forward for a closer look. "Why, good Lord, Stevens! It's Candace! An' she's been murdered— *shot square between the eyes!*"

16.

IT WAS A MOURNFUL PAIR who dismounted without haste at a little distance and moved forward for a closer examination. Sam's face was tight.

"This is the lowest I've seen yet," he ground out. "Killin' a girl—an' with Morgan in jail, too . . . There'll be nice news waitin' for him when he gets out!"

Pat said nothing, walking around the prone girl and continuing to look her over with care. When he straightened up to glance at Sam, the latter was utterly unprepared for the first words he spoke, quietly and deliberately.

"This girl isn't Candace Cowan, Sam."

"What—?" Sloan's stillness was marked. His sharp glance went to the girl's face once more. It was stained with dirt and blood, and positive identification was not easy; but of his own accord, he would never have voiced a doubt. "What makes yuh say that?" he jerked out incredulously.

"Look closer at her clothes," was the level answer.

"I see 'em." Sam was still mystified. "So what about it?"

"You never saw Candace wearin' that plaid skirt in her life," Pat pointed out. "She never wore gloves either. This girl's layin' on one—and there's the other one yonder."

Sam swore under his breath. It was like Stevens to take notice of these little items, plain enough now that they were pointed out. The average man would have failed to do so, as Sam had.

"Wal—" the latter scratched his grizzled thatch vigorously, with some show of relief. "Reckon you're right at that. I'm glad for Candace, anyway . . . But who *is* this girl that looks so much like her then, Stevens? An' what's she doin' here?"

129

Pat did not hurry over that one. "I think I know her. Maybe we can make sure . . . Take a look at that glove first. They're often marked—"

Sam walked over to pick up the glove out of the dust. Its size declared that none but a girl could have owned it. Sloan turned back the cuff, breaking stride as he did so.

"There is a name here," he exclaimed. "Kate S-h-a . . . Why, it's Jim Shaffer's girl!" His eyes darted again to the still body.

Sitting on one heel, Pat gazed away in grim thought.

Sam's own expression of perplexity slowly increased. "Shaffer lives only a couple o' miles south of here," he mused aloud. "Kate could've drifted over here easy enough. But how come anybody'd shoot her . . . Unless *they* mistook her for Candace too, mebby?"

Pat was already far beyond that point. "Most of Galloway's hands have been brought here from some other range," he said reflectively. "Only a few of 'em could have seen Candace more than twice—"

"Sure. An' that could go for any older man, too, for that matter."

"You're right." Pat nodded to himself. "Come to think of it, I'm not sure but I'm rather inclined to favor that slant."

Sam caught the direction of his thought. "But hell, Stevens! How could them hombres hope t' pin anything like this on Morgan while he's in jail?"

"They couldn't, of course." Pat's smile was tolerant. "But *we've* gone out of our way to write ourselves down as Ray Morgan's special cronies. Remember?"

Sam's jaw sagged. "Holy smoke! An' we've obliged 'em by ridin' over here an' findin' her." He broke off then, stubbornness in his manner. "It sure looks like our cue t' pull our freight fast, an' say nothin'. But I ain't doin' it."

"No," Pat assented at once. "We won't let Kate down. But there's no reason why we can't just happen to delay reportin' this for an hour or two longer, Sam," he added softly.

Sloan's glance darted to his face. "What are yuh thinkin' of?" he growled hopefully.

"Just a little rearrangement of details here." Pat's answer was curt. "I warned Galloway to expect the worst, and he's certainly got it comin' after this outrage. But probably he won't expect it quite so soon.''

Sam started for his horse, only to pause. "What about her—?" He guestured.

"We'll take that other glove along," Pat said practically, retrieving it from under the body and stuffing it into his pocket, "But I odn't recommend movin' her an inch. Lawlor'll be interested in this—and we want him to be."

"Okay. Let's get movin'." Sam was already peering about them uneasiy.

"Sure. But take a look first in Morgan's shed," Pat directed. "See if yuh can't pick up a Star Cross iron."

One was not available, whatever Ray may have done with the one or two branding irons he must have had made. Finding an old running iron, Pat said it would do, and they struck off across the hills. Sober-faced and resolute, they were soon on Flagg range once more.

"Yearlin' calf, I reckon?" Sam queried as they pushed on with care, keeping to cover and making sure they were not observed.

Pat nodded. "One we can shove over onto Star Cross graze without too much trouble."

It took some hunting to locate an animal exactly suited to their purpose, but at last they spotted one wandering along a willowy creek bottom. Several minutes' search failed to turn up its mother in the immediate vicinity, and it seemed a safe bet the calf had recently been weaned.

"Fine," Pat muttered. "Drop a rope on that critter, Sam, and take off. I'll keep watch."

A pair of genuine rustlers could hardly have gone to work with more effective stealth. While Pat maintained a careful surveillance of their surroundings, the squat man snaked the calf out of the brush and hustled it off toward Morgan's range with all possible dispatch.

At one point Stevens spotted a distant puncher on his way across the range. He did not drift this way, and they lay low till he was gone from sight. Half an hour later saw them well onto Star Cross ground. After building a tiny fire in a hollow to heat the running iron, they threw the calf and Sam knelt by its side.

"Will I vent this Flagg brand?" he asked, pausing.

Pat shook his head. "Torture it into a rough Star Cross, near as yuh can,'" he instructed. "We want it to look like a botch job—"

Sam, who at need could work as expertly as any brand blotter alive, artistically created an overbrand that could hardly have been mistaken for anything else. The calf bawled and writhed. Nodding his satisfaction with the job, Pat whipped the hogging string off and watched the animal buckjump away.

"That's part of the job done," he commented. "Now to make it real good. The other half may not prove quite so easy. But it's got to be done."

Sam gazed at him dubiously. "Jest how far are yuh figurin' t' go with this business?" he inquired.

Pat's grin was brief. "Far enough so there can't be any mistake about it in Lawlor's mind."

"Oh. Wal, in that case—"

After dropping the running iron far enough from the ashes of the fire for it to have been an accident, they took to the horses again and turned back toward the Flagg ranch.

"We're after a Flagg-branded horse now, I reckon," hazarded Sloan.

"One with a broken shoe, if possible," Pat agreed. "It may be something of a chore to spook one out of Galloway's corrals."

But whether his morning visit had anything to do with it, they found it virtually impossible to proceed within a mile of the Flagg ranch without running into mounted men who might or might not be watchers. Although they succeeded in keeping out of sight, both realized that their plan was blocked at least for the present.

Sam urged a prudent retreat. "We're licked, Stevens," he argued. "There ain't no gettin' though them hombres—let alone back again!"

Pat failed to reply, watching a rider who jogged off across the range alone, like a man on an errand. "Maybe we don't need to hunt any farther," he said slowly.

Sloan glanced the way he was looking. "I see." He was sententious. "Yuh figure we can snag that juniper—an' help ourselves to his bronc—"

"Take another look." Pat grinned. "It's not only a Flagg

horse, Sam—but unless I'm much mistaken, it's that rangy buckskin stallion that Mace rides occasionally. Could yuh improve on that?''

Keeping to cover and circling rapidly, they were able to intercept the Flagg man while he was crossing a corner of Morgan's Star Cross range. To their surprise as they rode boldly forward, it proved to be no less a person than Pike Tigart, the crusty Flagg foreman.

Tigart regarded them warily as they closed in. ''I got nothin' to say to yuh, Stevens,'' he barked. ''Yuh might just as well shove along.''

Pat did not even bother to answer, and it was Sam who spoke. ''What'll we do with 'im, Stevens?'' he asked, sober-faced. ''It's a plain case o' trespass, here on Morgan's grass—''

''We might make him walk,'' Pat responded, as if talking about someone not present. ''Maybe that'll make it stick in his mind next time.''

Tigart strove to whirl his horse away but it was already too late. Reaching out swiftly, Pat clamped an iron grip on the stallion's headstall. Sam closed in from the other side, and his bold stare probed Pike's rugged features coldly.

''Yeh?'' he purred invitingly. ''Yuh were sayin'—?''

Hard-bitten as he was, Tigart stayed his hand with stern self-repression in this sudden emergency. Despite their light-ness of tone, he did not underestimate this pair for an instant. They could be dynamite, as he had already found out.

Tigart's tone was flat and deadly with rage. ''I dunno what yore game might be, boys—but cut it short,'' he rasped out stiffly.

''Sure. We'll do that.'' Almost casually Sloan leaned forward and slugged him alongside the ear. ''I'll even save yuh the trouble of liftin' yore leg,'' Sam said as the Flagg man doubled out of the saddle to bring up on the ground.

Scrambling away from the stallion's restless heels, Tigart had all he could do to keep from jerking his gun. The impulse surged strong in his soul, and his fingers worked convulsively. Pat was watching narrowly his slightest move.

''Yuh'll pay for this, Stevens!'' Pike choked out, his leathery face congested.

''I'll chance it.'' Pat's retort was icy. ''Just hope yuh don't overreach yourself, Tigart.''

With a jerk of his head, he signaled to Sam. The seething foreman watched them turn away, Stevens leading the riderless buckskin. Without haste they jogged off in the general direction of the Lazy Mare.

But once well out of sight of the man they had set afoot, they swung rapidly round on their course, first making for the point at which they had overbranded the calf. Swinging into Tigart's vacated saddle, Pat made certain clear tracks there which he was satisfied would be plain reading to the next man who visited this spot, however he might misinterpret their significance. He started directly for the Star Cross then, while Sam hung back with the other horses, and continued his thoughtful work in the dust of Morgan's yard, ending up by removing his own and Sam's tracks with a branch of mesquite brush.

Finished, he waved at Sam. They turned Tigart's buckskin loose, chasing it in the general direction of the Flagg range, where it would eventually be picked up. Finally they set out for town.

"It could've been a mistake, draggin' Tigart into this set-up," She remarked, glancing across at his companion.

Pat evinced no uneasiness on that score. "A thorough acquaintance with Jess Lawlor's one-track mind has been useful to me before this," he returned. "I'm playing a long shot today, Sam. If it doesn't go off like a firecracker, as I expect, it won't work at all. So don't worry about it."

His chief concern, as he rode into Dutch Springs an hour later, was dispelled when he saw Sheriff Lawlor step into the jail office. The lawman was available. Pat slid out of the saddle and tossed his reins to Sam.

"This is it," he commented briefly. "See yuh later—"

Lawlor looked up from his desk at Pat's entrance. A shade of annoyance crossed his rugged face which he forebore to express save in the mildest terms.

"What now, Stevens?" he asked colorlessly.

Pat pretended great reluctance. "Sorry to bring this to yuh, Jess," he said. "I'm afraid things've gone pretty far this time—"

"Well. Out with it!" The lawman's irritation increased. "Seems to be yore purpose in life to bring me grief. What is it now?"

"Something or other seems to be goin' on over on young Morgan's range," Pat told him. "I didn't try too hard to learn what, for fear of coverin' tracks, Jess. But Sam and I did see what looks like a dead girl layin' in Morgan's ranch yard . . . yuh know Candace Cowan's been working over there off and on to help keep the place together for Ray," he reminded the Sheriff.

His features stiffening. Lawlor fired out a number of severe questions. Pat as promptly grew reticent, however. "As I say, I didn't do much nosing around, Jess," he said innocently. "I knew you'd be wantin' a report right off."

Lawlor strapped on his cartridge belt and took down hat and mackinaw jacket. "I'll ride out there," he growled. "I may want to talk to yuh, Stevens, when I get back."

"I'll be around."

Lawlor barged out without a backward look. Sam was waiting when Pat emerged from the jail at a more leisurely pace. "Man, he's sure burnin' up the brush." He gestured after the Sheriff. "Yuh didn't come right out an' *tell* him it was Candace, layin' out there at the Star Cross, did yuh?"

"I may have put some such idea in his head." Pat was unwontedly sober. "Dirty trick, maybe. But it can't hurt Kate now, for a day."

"What'll yuh do now, Stevens?" Sam was curious.

"Wait."

They were heading down for the comfortable chairs on the hotel porch when they saw Mace Galloway enter the Gold Eagle. They exchanged glances, and Sam's full lips were pursed.

"Better have ourselves a drink, hadn't we?" he murmured.

They racked their broncs, and stepped into the saloon. Galloway turned at the bar to glance toward them pompously. His gaze holding on Steven's face, he broke into a low chuckle.

"Well! Here's my shadow now," he rumbled good-humoredly. "Except I can't go far from here out, without stumblin' over you. Ain't figurin' on havin' me throwed in jail, are yuh, Stevens?"

The man had a presence, and he commanded considerable authority of manner. Jake, the bartender, discreetly grinned with him, Galloway's closing jibe being obviously the most farfetched the rancher could bring to mind.

Pat had his answer ready. "Hadn't thought of it, Mace—but I will," he promised coolly. "It might simplify matters, at that."

He and Sam moved to a table, from whence they idly followed Galloway's boasting talk. Waving a cigar expansively, the latter appeared utterly at his ease, drawing various acquaintances into conversation and thoroughly enjoying himself. The glances he occasionally tossed Pat were slyly malicious. No doubt he was thoroughly aware of the damage which had been done at the other's Lazy Mare ranch last night and was privately laughing up his sleeve.

"What a poisonality," Sam muttered in disgusted fashion. "Do me good t' cut that swelled pup down a few sizes."

Pat's expression was bland. He did not appear unduly disturbed. Yet he spent a good portion of his time glancing down the street through the window. The afternoon waned, and Sheriff Lawlor did not appear. Suppertime came, and Mace Galloway strolled across to the hotel. After eating he came back as cockily, replete and smiling.

"Waitin' for something?" he asked Pat, with obvious guile.

If Sam was boiling, Pat did not so much as deign a response to this manifest attempt at needling him. Glancing past the window again, he unconsciously straightened. Jess Lawlor came striding wearily down the street, making straight as an arrow for the Gold Eagle.

Galloway saw him enter. "Howdy, Jess," he called out heartily. "Been busy today, eh? Come an' wet yore whistle."

Striding forward bleakly, Lawlor laid a heavy hand on his arm. "Not now, Galloway. Sorry. Yuh'll have to come along . . . I'm takin' yuh in for Candace Cowan's murder."

Mace fell back, his face suddenly ashen. "Murder?" He gasped. "Jess—what in tophet is this all about?"

"Wal, I'll remind yuh if that's necessary. Yuh caught the Cowan girl overbrandin' one of yore calves, Galloway—killed her, and packed her over to Morgan's place, where yuh dumped her in his yard." Lawlor's rolling tone was final. "No use arguin', Mace, because I tracked yore hoss, that big buckskin with the busted calk. Come along."

17.

"HOLD ON THERE, LAWLOR! Hang it all, now!" For once Galloway was at a complete loss. "What in the world would I be up to any such crazy capers for? Besides, I've been in town all day. I can prove it!" His protest was vehement, but to little effect, if Lawlor's iron face was any criterion.

Pat quietly rose from his seat to move forward. He spoke up. "You weren't here his mornin'. Galloway, when I found yuh at your ranch!"

Mace's flaring glance ran to Pat's face, and caught. The angry blood churned back into his taut features with a rush. "By Jove! *You're* behind this rotten business, Stevens!" he choked. "I see it all now!"

"That's right," Pat grunted in masterful indifference to this attack. "Morgan's well out of the way, so blame your dirty work on me, Mace—I'm next handiest!"

In Lawlor's mind at least, it was a telling retort. To his credit, it must be admitted that the crime appeared a particularly heinous one. Thorough-going enough in his stolid way, the lawman had read the sign on the range as Pat had wanted him to. It had not occurred to him to question Pat's adroitly planted suggestion as to the girl's identity. In Lawlor's straightforward, plodding life few acts had gone against the grain more bitterly than the stern duty which he saw confronting him now. Yet he did not hesitate.

"Come on, Galloway." His hamlike hand closed on the man's shoulder and heaved impellingly.

Still the Flagg rancher stubbornly balked. "Dammit, Jess,

I ain't runnin' off nowheres! Give me a chance to say two words—!''

It was gall to the lawman to be forced to argue with this friend of whose guilt he was unfortunately well satisfied. "Save it, man. This'll be thrashed over aplenty before they get around to hangin' yuh!''

Mace blanched at Lawlor's closing phrase. The look he darted at Stevens then was pure venom. In some bewilderment, his glance ran on around the hard faces in the place. The men in the Gold Eagle muttered ominously, glaring in his direction with freezing contempt.

"But, Jess, I *swear* I didn't kill no girl!'' Brief panic rang in the rising ejaculation. "What kind of a fool would I be t' do such a thing, even if I did catch the Cowan girl overbrandin' one of my calves?''

"Wal, near's I can make out, she was doin' it for young Morgan,'' Lawlor returned stonily. "Seems to me that puts a different face on it—''

"So what?'' Galloway panted, frantically grasping at meagerest hope in his desperation. "Tryin' my best to get Red to work for me, wasn't I? I was only too willin' to help the boy build up his herd!''

Ezra had stepped into the place a few moments ago. "Phooey!'' he burst out gruffly, with some show of repugnance. "What stinks in here?'' He glanced deliberately at Galloway. "No soap, Mace,'' he said then, flatly. "Morgan wants no part of yuh—an' we all know how yuh felt about that! Unless Pike Tigart was actin' flat against yore orders, he's been mighty busy buildin' the boy's herd—backwards!'' He broke off to glare. "If there's any doubt, we kin all go down to the jailhouse now an' ask Morgan whether yuh hate his guts!''

Other men were crowding into the saloon as word spread quietly around town. More than one of them snarled at Galloway, venting their contempt for a man who could bring himself to shoot a young girl.

"I'm tellin' yuh, Lawlor! This whole thing is Stevens's work!'' Mace broke out in a fury. "I don't know what kind of hocus-pocus he used on yuh—but dig deep enough and you'll find it! He rode to my place this mornin' and as much as warned me of a double-cross! I laughed at him . . . If I'd knowed the rat better, I'd have called you in then!''

"Bah. We don't wanta hear no more!" a defiant voice exclaimed. Not one of these men but knew Stevens better than they did Galloway. "Haul him in, Jess, before we take a chore off the judge's hands—"

Accepting the hint for what it was undoubtedly worth, Lawlor began to haul the still resisting rancher toward the door. Galloway got a rough jostling from these angry men, but the Sheriff succeeded in getting him outside. They headed without loss of time for the jail.

Sam Sloan watched them depart, at last turning to rejoin Pat and Ezra. There was blank wonder in the gleam of his eye. "Wal, Stevens. Yuh might as well explain this phony deal to us now," he muttered under his breath.

Pat motioned them over to a table where they were by themselves. "Keep your voice down," he warned. "You now I've been dealin' off the bottom for reasons of my own."

"Sure. I know." Sam was insistent, still obviously mystified. "But, Pat, we found out that dead girl *wasn't* Candace—"

"If I'm right, Galloway knows it, too," Pat cut him off. "But right now he's plenty worried. We'll let him sleep on it, and see what happens."

"But, hang it, others're bound t' find out—includin' Lawlor!"

"But maybe not soon enough to save Galloway," returned Pat evenly.

Sam shook his head dubiously. "You're walkin' a tightrope," he said thinly. "Lawlor sent Dade an' Henry Martin out t' pick up that girl." Martin was the Dutch Springs coroner. "Old Cowan'll be called in tomorrow to make the identification. The cat'll be out of the bag then, if not sooner."

Pat shrugged. "There's the flaw in my plan, square under your finger," he admitted frankly. "If Galloway doesn't crack before morning, he won't at all. I'm gambling that he will."

Ezra had been taking all this in with knit brows. "It's all blame nigh Chinese t' me," he grumbled finally. "Suppose yuh let me in on it, if it's *that* good—"

As briefly as possible, Pat posted him on the events of the day. Ezra whistled soundlessly, his one eye glinting.

"Things're comin' to a head fast," he murmured. "Dunno what you're anglin' for, Stevens, but I'll back the play. What'll yuh do now?"

"Keep an eye on things." Pat was offhand. "Not much else to do now but mark time."

They heard many heated discussions of Mace Galloway's supposed crime as the evening dragged on. At a late hour, a hubbub out in the street advised them that something was going on, and they moved out there. The late arrival in town of coroner and deputy, with their grim burden packed on an extra horse, was drawing considerable attention.

Pat and the partners watched the remains of the unfortunate girl being carried into the little shack where Henry Martin also ran an assay office. Men strove to crowd in there, without success. The door shut with a slam of finality and Rufe Dade led the horses away. Sam grunted.

"Reckon they ain't found out yet who she is," he murmured hopefully.

Pat's nod expressed his satisfaction. "No need of hurryin' Jim Shaffer's grief along. He's probably worried to death now by Kate's absence." He started to turn away. "See you boys in the morning, I expect—"

"Sure, yuh will." Ezra looked at him suspiciously. "Where yuh going'?"

Pat waved toward the jail. "Little job I shouldn't overlook—"

They watched while he strode down there and stepped in the door. Lawlor and Rufe Dade were alone in the office, evidently conferring. They glanced up at him suspiciously.

"Yeh, Stevens?" the Sheriff accosted him queryingly.

Pat's nod was disarming. "Go ahead, Jess. Listenin' to Rufe's report, I expect . . . Just thought I'd stick around for a while—"

"The hell yuh will, Stevens!" The cadaverous deputy was openly hostile. He had never taken a shine to Pat, being just dull-witted enough to mistrust the other. "*I'm* guardin' the jail tonight. I don't need no company!"

Pat spread his hands. "Of course, you're the doctor, Jess,"

he told Lawlor, ignoring Dade's blustering authority. "It just occurred to me that Galloway's crowd might show up and maybe try to spring him . . . You wouldn't hear a word against Mace a day or two ago," he went on artlessly. "It didn't change the facts any. Maybe now you'll be warned in time."

Lawlor rasped his jaw, his glance travelling to his deputy's lean horse-face. "Didn't even think of that, for a fact," he allowed thoughtfully. He half-turned away then. "Do as you're a mind to, Stevens. I needn't warn yuh not to be foolish enough to make any mistakes."

Pat smiled at the scowling deputy. "Me and Rufe always got along," he assured the lawman blandly.

"Yeh. Yore way," Dade muttered, not at all pleased.

Lawlor ignored them and moved into the cell block, where Galloway and young Morgan were locked in opposite cells. He made sure that everything was all right, then returned.

"Reckon I'll have a confab with Henry. Keep folks out of here now, Rufe, for yore own good." He left a moment later, bending his steps toward the coroner's shack.

Silence settled down on the jail office. Dade installed himself grumpily at the Sheriff's desk without speech, and Pat stretched out on a bench against the wall. It was warm in here after the nipping night air, and he presently fell into dreamy meditation.

Galloway proved restless in his cell. The silence must have borne heavily on him. "Lawlor!" he called harshly at the end of ten minutes.

Dade was short with him. "Dry up, Galloway! Lawlor ain't here."

"I don't care if he ain't." Mace was ugly. "I demand a lawyer. Better get one in here pronto, or I'll make it hot for yuh when he does come!"

"Yuh'll get a lawyer. Tomorrow," Rufe called back, with brutal frankness. "Where'll yuh find one that'll worry about yore troubles at this hour?"

"Wal, I'll make it worth his while, don't fret. I want somebody—and fast," Galloway insisted, with a return of his old arrogance. "Send out to the ranch, Dade. I want Pike Tigart in here, and I want him tonight. Yuh understand?"

It was only the beginning of Galloway's truculent demands as the night wore on. He became increasingly loud as his trials grew on him. Knowledge of far-flung guilt rested heavily enough on his mind, without his being accused of a piece of rank folly which he was painfully conscious of never having perpetrated.

"Blast it all, Dade," he roared. "Yuh think yuh got me short-hauled now, but yuh'll all sweat for this foolishness before it's over!"

Ray Morgan had been listening to this extended tirade in silence, hoping to discover the reason for Mace's incarceration, no word of Candace's supposed death having been allowed to reach his ear. But at last he boiled over with scornful disgust.

"For Lord's sake, Galloway!" he hurled through the bars at the other man. "Will yuh put a snaffle on that lip of yours, and let a man get some rest?"

In the office, Pat raised his head at this, listening alertly. Galloway was silent for a space, gathering his forces. He let go explosively.

"Go t' hell, Morgan! This whole thing is yore fault for foolin' around with that girl in the first place, and bein' such a lunkhead!"

The electricity generated by this speech could almost be felt, as Ray turned it over in his smoking thoughts. "What girl is that, Galloway?" he rasped. "What are yuh drivin' at, anyway?"

Mace's silence became pronounced as his position dawned on him. Morgan wa credited with being sweet on the girl he stood accused of murdering. Contemptuous of the younger man as he professed to be, he was not sorry the bars stood between them.

"Come on—out with it, will yuh!" Ray yelled at him, thoroughly aroused now. "What girl would you be referrin' to, mister—and what about her?"

"I got nothin' to say to yuh, Morgan." Galloway's tone was gruffly reluctant. "Leave me alone, now."

With a show of exhausted patience, Rufe Dade listened gloweringly to this heated exchange without offering interference.

Pat succeeded in catching the deputy's eye. "Better put a stop to that, Dade," he murmured significantly, "while there's time."

"Oh, keep quiet, Stevens," returned Rufe half-savagely. "Or I'll end up by throwin' yuh out of here—"

He had to raise his voice to be heard over Morgan's surcharged tones, issuing from the dark cell block. Ray was giving vent to his feelings by cursing the unscrupulous rancher with all the fervor at his command.

"*You're* the one who's draggin' some girl into this, Mace Galloway, and I aim to know what's behind it," he bawled.

The abrupt crash of a gunshot racketed through the confining walls. It came from the cell block. So alertly keyed was Pat that he was off the bench and halfway to the door before the astonished Dade could get his legs under him.

"What in hell's that?" Rufe brought out in a growl.

"Galloway must have been packin' a hidden gun," snapped Pat. "He's tryin' to finish off Morgan with it . . . Stay back, now, till I settle this!"

The rawboned deputy would have interfered, but he was too late. Pat slipped into the cell block and crouched in protective darkness as another echoing shot crashed out. He heard Morgan's yell and his feet scrambling in the cell opposite Galloway's.

"Mace," Pat called out piercingly. "Drop that gun! Kick it through the bars—before I search every corner of that cell with lead!"

So fierce was Galloway's rage against the helpless puncher in the opposite cell that he fired a third time, seeking to strike the other down by means of a lucky shot. Pat's own gun roared and the slug bounced off a steel grate, to whine wickedly through Galloway's narrow cubicle. That brought him to his senses.

"Hold it, Stevens!" he croaked anxiously. "I'm done. I won't shoot no more!"

Pat grunted. "Different, when you're the one on the receiving end, eh? . . . Let me hear that gun slide out here."

The weapon grated across the floor. Pat groped for it and got it.

"Morgan," he called tensely. "Are yuh all right?"

"No thanks to Galloway, if I am," Ray's angry exclamation sounded promptly. "Why don't yuh drag that treacherous wolf out and string him up?"

Such an opening was Pat's chance, and he did not pass it up. "That'll probably happen," he tossed out unemotionally. "Once it's learned that, after all he's accused of already, Mace has gone hog-wild and tried to kill a man in his cell."

It sounded utterly damning. Assured that the danger of flying lead was past, Dade came bustling in with a lantern. Galloway slumped in his cell, crushed.

"Morgan was drivin' me crazy with his damned chatter," he exclaimed defensively. "By right I shouldn't even be in here—" He was shivering now as if with ague.

Nobody bothered to contradict him. Dade looked both his prisoners over, ascertaining that Morgan had fortunately escaped injury. He silently motioned Pat outside. Following, he closed the cell-block door with a slam.

"Let 'em rot," was his callous ultimatum.

Pat more accurately judged the extent of mental torture under which the Flagg rancher labored for the duration of the night. He was unfeignedly relieved when, early the following morning, Sam Sloan put in an appearance accompanied by Sheriff Lawlor.

Jess's glance slid to Pat. "Everything quiet?"

"Quiet!" echoed Dade disgustedly. He threw back the cell-block door. "Yuh can listen for yoreself—"

Jess heard a cracked and rusty voice. "Lawlor!" It was Galloway, and he sounded urgent. "Come on, Lawlor! I want yuh in here!"

Lawlor calmly moved that way, shucking his coat. Pausing to hang it on a hook, he was arrested by a glimpse of Mace's flushed and determined face through the bars.

"What's botherin' you, Galloway?"

"Let me out." Mace's rushing words were a counterpart of his decided manner. Evidently he had fully made up his mind during the night, and he left no doubt as to his decision. "I've had more than enough of this! That girl yuh picked up *couldn' tve'* been the Cowan girl!" he declared doggedly. "I'll prove it, and yore whole story'll fall flat!"

Lawlor had come armed this morning with the knowledge

that the dead girl was not Candace, but, held by a faint surprise, he failed to mention it. Curiosity made him gruff.

"How'll yuh prove that?" he asked slowly.

Galloway's answer electrified them all. "Because I'm prepared to show her to yuh, alive and kickin'," he shot back triumphantly. "Shall we get goin'?"

Sam's eyes were the size of saucers. "Mighty cute of yuh, Stevens," he muttered in an aside to Pat, under cover of Morgan's vehement exclamations. "How in Hannah did yuh know *he* had Candace tucked away some'eres?"

Pat could afford to be casual, now that his long gamble had paid off. He shrugged. "It was a good guess."

18.

COME ON, LAWLOR! Unlock this cell!" It was more like an
order than a plea. Galloway gestured across toward Morgan.
"I've put up with that all night, and I'm sick of it!"

Jess had the jail keys in his hand, yet he hesitated. "If yuh
knew the Cowan girl was alive, why didn't yuh put up yore
kick last night?" he demanded shrewdly.

"Kick!" Mace snorted wrathfully. "How loud does a man
have to kick before yuh'll hear it?" But he understood what
the lawman was driving at. "Don't worry, Lawlor! I'll show
yuh that girl, and no tricks about it, My neck's worth that
much to me—"

Lawlor appeared hard to convince. While he was fumbling
unhurriedly with the cell lock, Morgan unleashed a hot blast
at him.

"Be careful what you're lettin' yoreself in for, Sheriff,"
he blazed. "If that skunk can take yuh straight to Candace
Cowan, then her father's charge against me sure falls down!
Either I go along with yuh, or this is a case of fake arrest—
and neither you nor Cowan'll be able to forget it!"

The lawman turned back to gaze at him in frowning perplexity. Sam Sloan's laugh was harsh. "He's got an argument there." His smooth comment was a subtle taunt. "How
many men *are* responsible for the girl's disappearance,
anyhow?"

"Slack away, Morgan," Jess growled, beginning to lose
his temper. "It ain't no sure thing Galloway's tellin' the
truth. But if we do find the girl, you'll be out of that cell as
soon afterward as I'm able t' manage it."

"I will—not!" Ray was stern. "From what's been said

here, Galloway's tryin' to duck a murder rap. Either he's lyin' now, or I'm innocent of kidnappin'! You're givin' me the same chance yuh give him, or there'll be a new sheriff in this man's town!''

His contention appeared sound enough to the most stubborn mind. Lawlor weighed the matter grumpily. "Where is the girl, Galloway?" he rasped.

Mace showed a significant reticence. "No, yuh don't, Lawlor! I ain't tellin' yuh nothin'! I'll take yuh there, and that's all I'll do."

Pat pretended to voice a reluctant persuasion. "You'll have to let Morgan out, Lawlor," he said in a low tone. "There's no other way. He can come along under guard—"

"*Galloway*'ll go under guard—not me," Ray promptly fired out, with truculent insistence. "I'll be damned if he gets another chance to knock me off, and that's flat!"

"Huh?" The Sheriff scented a mystery. "What's this?"

"Oh, Mace lost his head last night," Pat supplied indifferently, not wanting anything to block their progress, now that Galloway had cracked. "We straightened him out fast enough."

Lawlor looked at the rancher strangely, as if never having rightly seen him before. "In that case, we'll give him a thorough search before any more—accidents happen." He threw Galloway's cell open. "Frisk him good, Rufe."

The deputy roughly complied, much to Mace's disgruntlement, while Jess proceeded to release Morgan. The young redhead stepped out of his cell with obvious relief. He glanced steadily at Pat.

"This must be your doin', Stevens," he muttered stiffly. "I don't know how yuh managed it—but I'll give yuh the benefit of the doubt."

Pat grinned easily. "Well, it could be that Galloway did yuh a favor without knowin' it," he discounted lightly. "We'll see what he comes up with."

Ray nodded. Having seen the Lazy Mare man in action, he was not deceived. That he could maintain as firm a grip on this situation as anyone was attested a moment later.

"Snap the cuffs on that man, Lawlor," he ordered, indicating Galloway as they stepped out of the cell block. "He's still under suspicion of murder, as I reminded yuh before.

We're certain to run into his friends, and then it might be too late.''

Mace fumed and snarled, blowing his threats at such uncalled-for manhandling. But Lawlor was commencing to harbor his own reasons for doubting the man's integrity. ''Morgan's right, Galloway. Give the devil his due,'' he jested grimly as he clamped the bracelets on the exasperated rancher. ''Personally, I hope you're able to produce the girl. Till yuh do, I'm obliged to take precautions.''

That the matter would not end there he neglected to state. Galloway's anxiety to get out from under a preposterous charge was so strong that he apparently failed to realize the fact. Pat was the only one who read his true motive. Mace was willing to make any sacrifice to get out, counting on his sharp wits to serve him thereafter.

Sam and Rufe Dade lost no time in getting up the horses. There were six in the little group that pulled away from the jail a few minutes later. It was too early to attract public attention, though undoubtedly they were seen. Galloway set their direction, and it was lost on no one that they seemed to be heading straight for the Flagg range. Ray Morgan had been allowed to proceed without encumbrance, though it was noticeable that the lanky deputy sheriff rode close to him most of the time. It did not appear to bother the young fellow, and Sam was able unobtrusively to post him on recent events. Ray whistled softly at the end, staring at Galloway's back.

''Takin' a crack at your Bar ES horses—tryin' to finish Stevens off—and here's this business about Candace,'' he muttered in amazement. ''Galloway's sure gone overboard! Or else he's got more confidence in himself that I have . . . Mean to tell me Lawlor ain't wise to all this?''

Sam smiled. ''Stevens is pretty good at skinnin' skunks. If Mace ain't guessed the knife's been slipped into his hide already, I'm disappointed in him.''

Galloway was leading them across the remote corner of the Flagg range now. It was cold today. Collars were turned up. There was a raw wind, and a storm seemed to be brewing. The sky was leaden, heavy, unpromising.

A couple of miles west of Flagg headquarters, Galloway

drew rein in a fringe of pines. "Wait here, Lawlor, and I'll bring the girl to yuh," he proposed boldly. "It won't take me fifteen minutes. I've still got these cuffs on, and I won't be foolish enough to run—"

Jess blinked at him owlishly. "Are yuh serious?" he growled, not bothering to wait for an answer. His tone hardened. "Either take us to the girl like yuh said or, Galloway, we're headin' back for that jail, here an' now."

Mace displayed a disposition to argue. "Blast it all, Jess! Yuh've known me for quite a while—" he began weightily.

Jess's headshake was adamant. "I don't know what you're aimin' to hide. But I ain't bargainin', Galloway. I want to see the Cowan girl!"

Morgan himself could not have put it more aptly and forcibly. Glancing around at these bleak faces, Mace seemed to understand that he was licked.

"All right—come on," he snarled, wheeling his horse. "We'll get this over with."

A great part of his upper range was covered with broken forest, a land fanged with rocks and gashed by hidden canyons. Gusts of wind soughed dismally in the upper branches as they started off through the pines, and fugitive snowflakes began to sift down.

Galloway followed an angling trail down a steep canyonside. Before long Pat glimpsed a red-walled log cabin below. Thickening snow slanted across the intervening space, but he saw the adjacent corral and two or three horses stamping about within. Morgan saw it, too. His face tightened at the prospect of presently finding Candace.

They reached the canyon floor and pushed on, Lawlor scanning the cabin with interest. A wisp of smoke issued from its rough stone chimney.

"One of yore stock camps, I take it," he remarked colorlessly.

"Take it any way yuh want," snarled Mace, rendered savage by the necessity of what he was doing. "I'm undertakin' to turn that girl over to yuh, Lawlor—and then you'll turn me loose, and no monkey business about it!"

No such terms had been included in their dubious bargain, but the Sheriff said nothing. None of them was inclined to

pause for discussion at this juncture. If Mace thought he
would presently see the end of his entanglement, however, he
was due for a disappointment.

"Man, if Candace is only here, will I rub Cowan's nose in
the dirt!" Ray exclaimed under his breath. But Pat deemed
the young fellow honestly more concerned for the girl herself
than for anything else. Morgan could hardly contain his
impatience.

"Hello—Jake!" Galloway hailed the cabin as they drew up
before the place.

After a moment's wait, the slab door jarred open on a
crack. A man peeped out, and there was a further delay
before he crowded through to face them, pulling the door to
behind him jealously. Sam gaped at him incredulously. It was
Pike Tigart.

The crabbed Flagg foreman looked at his employer narrowly, his sour glance touching the others and withdrawing.
"Yeh?" he growled shortly. "What yuh want?" He seemed
trying, by this manner at least, to convey a warning.

Galloway stared at him with reddening features. "Wal,
Pike!" He was gruff. "What are you doin' here?"

Tigart shrugged. "Jake needed a breather," he muttered
against his will. "I'm expectin' him back anytime—"

His stolid mind was cautiously feeling out the reason for
the presence here of Sheriff Lawlor and the others. Pat Stevens's appearance struck him as particularly ominous, wary
as he was of tricks. But Galloway brushed this aside.

"All right, Tigart." He was short. "Since you're here, trot
that girl out—"

For a brief space the foreman did not move, his jaw slowly
sagging. Not for an instant had he so much as dreamed that
Galloway's companions might even suspect her presence. To
state the fact thus baldly seemed to him sheer madness. His
mouth snapped shut. "Do you know what you're doin',
Mace?" he demanded harshly.

Morgan's unwavering blue eyes were ablaze. "You heard
your boss, Tigart," he rapped out. "If Candace is in that
shack, get her out here!"

Still Tigart hesitated, unwilling to accept what was happening. "Mace—" he began hoarsely.

"Dammit, man!" Galloway was apoplectic. "I've been accused to my face of murderin' that girl! . . . Do yuh think I *don't* know what I'm doin'?"

Tigart went pasty. His hand shook as he started to open the door. "Okay—if I'm actin' under orders," he mumbled. "But I don't want nothin' t' do with this!"

The words were a mistake. It was then Stevens privately concluded that Tigart had had only too much to do with the matter. He filed the thought away, for use at its proper time.

Pike was gone from view for the space of three or four minutes, while Morgan fidgeted in the saddle. Without ostentation Sam moved around behind Galloway, keeping his every movement in sight. The slab door scraped back, and Candace Cowan stood in the opening, unharmed but considerably harassed, if her expression meant anything. Suddenly it altered.

"Ray!" she cried. "I knew you would come for me—!"

Out of the saddle in a twinkling, Morgan had her hands in his. It was all he could do to keep from taking her in his arms.

Mace Galloway's rasping words brought them back to earth with a jar. "There yuh are, Lawlor," the rancher ground out with all his old arrogance. "And there's your murder charge, flat as a pancake! Suppose yuh get these trinkets off me, and be quick about it!" He lifted the handcuffs.

"Oh, I dunno," Sam cut in sarcastically. "What about this kidnappin' rap, Lawlor, that was strong 'nough t' hold Morgan on? Or don't it apply to Big Britches here—" He indicated Galloway with exaggerated deference.

"No, yuh don't!" Mace's voice rose with the rigidity of steel. "Lawlor, I'm warnin' yuh now. There's a limit to how far yuh can go with me. Don't crowd me! You've got that girl, safe an' sound. Take a tip! Turn me loose and clear out!"

"Hold it, boys." Pat's levelness of tone was enough to arrest them all. "Let's not get mixed up. We've found Candace—but there's still that dead girl to be explained away. It can't be done in a minute."

"Shaffer's girl, yuh mean." Lawlor nodded. "I know."

On the verge of an outburst, Galloway paused, arrested his

dead glance stealing to the Sheriff's face. "Yuh mean yuh let me lead yuh here—knowin' all the time it was another girl that was killed?" he whipped out.

Jess nodded woodenly. "There was this charge against Morgan," he returned dryly. "Long as there was a chance of disprovin' it I had to play along—and it seems I did, with Pat Stevens's help." It was a magnificent concession for him, even if Galloway did not appear to appreciate it.

"I'm not done with this murder charge, either," Pat inserted. He broke off to dive out of the saddle and nail Tigart to the ground as the foreman made an attempt to scuttle around the corner of the cabin and slip away. "Easy, Tigart," he admonished disgustedly, hauling the other up. "Wouldn't be laborin' under a guilty conscience, would yuh?"

"Why should I?" Tigart blustered huffily, striving to break free without success. "Take yore paws off me, Stevens! I don't know what you're drivin' at—"

"Yes, you do," Pat assured cheerfully. "In fact, it's got something to do with your bein' here now."

Pike stiffened, blanching under his weathered tan. "H-how could that be? I only turned up here this mornin' by pure accident!" He seemed almost afraid of the answer, yet defiant.

Pat said, "You know only too well what happened to the Shaffer girl, Tigart. You were prowlin' around Morgan's Star Cross ranch when yuh spotted her there. *You* can't be bothered to tell one girl from another—a crusty old reprobate like you! . . . Yuh thought she was Candace." He never took his shrewd gaze off the foreman's face, driving on. "You new Candace was being held here—under Galloway's orders. Yuh thought she'd escaped; and if she had, that'd been just too bad for you. So you let her have it, Tigart—how could you know I was watchin' the whole thing?—and after sleepin' on it overnight, you rode out here hotfoot to see just how wrong yuh might be!"

Tigart visibly shrank as the grim indictment ran its inexorable course to the end. He seemed to fear Pat unreasonably, every line of his wizened face betraying the correctness of the other's surmise down to chapter and verse. His boss never gave him a chance to speak up.

"Yuh crazy fool!" Mace bellowed. "So it was *you* brought all this down on my head!"

Pat never let up on Tigart, shaking him sternly. "Speak up, man. It'll go worse with you if yuh don't." Every word was a blow. "Am I right or wrong?"

"Wal, I—I—" Gasping, Pike writhed in Pat's grip, seeing no way to turn. "Yes, I did it, Stevens . . . But it was an accident, I tell yuh! She grabbed at my gun! I swear I didn't mean—"

Waiting for no more, Pat turned toward Lawlor. "There's your case, Jess," he said levelly. "Discount Tigart's clumsy lies, and you have all the answers. I'll have more to say about Galloway when we get back to town. Better bring him along . . ."

He paused, noting the lawman's distraction. Lawlow gazed up the trail through the thickening snow as if he had ceased to listen. He was intent on something else, and as hushed silence descended over this pine-shrouded canyon glade, Sam Sloan caught an inkling of what it was.

"Somebody comin'," he muttered tightly. "Better step in the cabin here—"

"Too late, mister man."

A puncher rode out through the snow-dusted pines, a saturnine cast on his ruddy face. A carbine rested across his saddle. His obsidian pupils flickered over them all watchfully. Their blank surprise at this unheralded arrival was plain. Suddenly the carbine cracked flatly, and Rufe Dade hastily dropped his gun, rubbing his stinging fingers.

"Utah!" Galloway's voice was rich with surprised gratification. "Where's the boys?"

The man called Utah waved vaguely, a comprehensive gesture. "More or less all around yuh, boss," he drawled. His glance sharpened at the sight of the handcuffs. "Wouldn't be needin' some help right now, by any chance?"

Mace's laugh was guttural. "I could do with less company—not meanin' yourself," he allowed. "It's our friend Pike, there, who really needs yuh most. Got himself in a fine jackpot, he has!"

With the barrel of his gun, Utah waved Pate away from the foreman. His mouth a thin line, Pat glanced about. At least three other men were closing in on them, outlaws beyond a doubt.

"Do as he says, Stevens," murmured Sheriff Lawlor. "I never argue with a leveled gun. Rufe'll tell yuh—"

"And be sharp about it, too, Stevens!" Galloway threw in, expansive now that the tables were turned. "You're makin' my foreman mighty uneasy, standin' there. I wouldn't put it past him to resent it—if yuh know what I mean."

Silently, his gray eyes expressionless, Pat complied, moving toward his horse.

19.

"How's that suit yuh, Pike? Make yuh feel better?" Galloway grinned jovially at this weak jest, his rage against the
other man forgotton in his overwhelming relief. "Under the
circumstances, I don't reckon Stevens'll have any further
interest in yuh."

Mace moved toward Lawlor as he talked, motioning the
lawman down off his horse. Scowling, Jess slid stiffly to the
ground.

"Lift yore hands out of my way, Lawlor. About shoulder
height." He was thoroughly enjoying himself, boldly investi-
gating the other man's pockets in his search for the keys.
Breathing hard, Jess submitted under the steady, baleful eye
of a carbine-carrying renegade. At his moment there could
have been no angrier man in Powder County.

Pat read his bitter mood. For crucial days and weeks the
Sheriff had refused to believe in the remote possibility of
Mace Galloway's perfidy. It was all coming home to roost
now with pitiless force. Lawlor would never forget the lesson. How much it could help him now was an open question.

Mace found the keys. Hauling them out, he proceeded to
free himself from the handcuffs, tossing them carelessly aside.
"Ought to snap 'em on Stevens," he grunted. "But I'll do
better'n that."

"Let me go t' work on him," Utah urged, staring intently
at Pat, against whom he appeared to entertain an instinctive
antipathy. "He's a nosey hombre—"

Mace took his meaning, his eye dropping to the leveled
carbine. "No," he ruled promptly. "No use givin' some

U.S. Marshal a better cause for followin' us up, boys. I don't want no truck with the law—and Lawlor's a reasonable man.'' He grinned wolfishly. ''I aim to discourage this bunch. If I have to do it the hard way later on, that'll come, too.''

''Don't be makin' no mistakes now, Galloway!'' Tigart's exclamation was taut and hard. ''I warned yuh Stevens knows about Bluestem. He's been there. So has Morgan—an' this fat runt.'' He jerked a thumb at Sam. ''They're all a bull-headed crowd. Stop 'em cold an' be done with it!''

Candace gasped at this cool proposal of wholesale killing. Mace took his pleasure in scrutinizing their blank faces, as if toying with the idea. He had been brought up in a stern school; it was not beyond him to follow the dictates of self-preservation, regardless of where they led him. But with an avenue of escape open, he could be level-headed as well about the future.

''Shoot one, an' yuh might's well knock 'em all off,'' he declared dourly. ''But that skinny, one-eyed buzzard ain't here. I don't like it.'' He shook his head.

''Don't forget they downed Tex!'' the foreman interjected angrily. ''*I'd* make somebody sweat for that, an' be damned to 'em!''

''No doubt yuh would.'' Galloway was suavely firm. ''But I ain't forgettin' you're in a different boat from the rest of us . . . Not that I rightly blame yuh for wantin' us in there with yuh, Pike.'' There was acid in his impudent smirk. ''Tex took his chances—and from here out, so'll you.''

With a smooth movement, he lifted Sheriff Lawlor's six-gun and thrust it into his own empty holster. As methodically, he confiscated the weapons of the others, tossing them to a flat-faced confederate. Morgan too courageously made an attempt to thrust him angrily back, only to slip in the snow steadily gathering underfoot. One of the renegades as promptly banged him alongside the head with a rifle barrel. Ray staggered back, nursing the bruise.

''Hot-headed younger bugger,'' Mace remarked, adroitly tossing Morgan's Colt after the others. ''Gotta know how to handle a hedgehog.'' He turned to one of his silent men. ''Arkansas. Get some rope, there in the shack. I want yuh to tie Stevens up out here where I can see it. Pop'll help yuh.''

Arkansas brought the rope, a stout Manila lariat. He and the crease-faced old rawhide called Pop went methodically about trussing Pat in such a manner that he could hardly move a finger. "Humph!" Mace scrutinized the knots jealously, trying various strands of the rope for tightness. "Reckon that'll do . . . Lawlor's next."

Jess Lawlor's stiff-necked dignity found it impossible to submit to this indignity without severe protest. "You're only slammin' the door on yoreself, Galloway," he burst out forcefully, cheeks trembling.

Mace laughed indulgently. "So long as it stand between you and me, Lawlor, I won't kick."

So little troubled by scruples did the renegades appear that they bound that lawman even more roughly and firmly. With Stevens, he was dragged inside the cabin and tumbled to the floor. Sam was next, submitting in hard-eyed silence, his lips puffed out. Rufe Dade was similarly treated. Morgan watched the proceedings with steadily mounting hostility.

"Throw a rope over this girl, Galloway, and I'll follow yuh to hell!" he ejaculated with suppressed fury.

Mace's regard was cool. "Sho! I wouldn't think of it, boy. Can't be treatin' the ladies in any such shabby fashion." His tone was oily with delayed menace. "In fact," he added negligently, as some of the uneasiness faded from Morgan's face, "she's goin' to be our insurance—"

Alarm leaped afresh to Morgan's hard, flat cheeks. "Spell that out," he rasped.

"Yuh don't get it?" Mace's innocence was exaggerated. "Why, she's goin' along with us, Ray—just in case yuh should take a notion someday to crowd us too close."

Ray's lean features went fiery with desperation. For ten seconds his wrath made the air blue. "Where yuh takin' her?" he blazed.

Galloway shrugged. "Yuh may locate her again someday. She might even find her way back, if she feels up to it."

With the ropes already entangling his legs, Morgan lunged at him, his face murderous. Mace casually stepped aside, then flattened him with a heavy blow. His voice suddenly altered.

"Tie him good," he growled. "Stuff a gag in his chops."

He grew busy taking a final look at Pat and Sheriff Lawlor, and glancing about the cabin. "Shake it up, will yuh? We're gettin' out of here!"

Her face bloodless, the girl stared at him, standing alone in the center of the cabin. Galloway avoided her eye, tossing her coat at her carelessly. "Climb into that—and whatever else yuh can find," he snapped. "It'll be rough goin' today."

Numbly she followed instructions. Pat watched her with concern as long as she remained in sight. Galloway lost no time in thrusting her outside, and the renegades followed, leaving the slab door aswing.

"Better pull that door to," they heard Utah's grating mutter, drifting in through the opening. "Somebody's liable t' find 'em too quick—if they get t' yellin'."

"Let it go." Galloway's response was curt. "Nobody'll be cruisin' in this storm. With the door open, the cold'll do as good a job as a gun—and it can't be chalked up to us."

Their lowered voices died out. Snow swirled in over the cabin threshold, and chill gusts drove smoke down the chimney. In the hushed silence, the five bound men lay listening to the faint sounds of hasty departure from outside. These ceased with the dying out of sodden hoof stamps. The silence was heavier than ever. Sloan was the first to find his voice.

"Galloway hit it plumb center," he growled at last. "We'll freeze in here, soon's that fire dies down—"

Jess Lawlor heaved about ineffectually, tugging at his bonds. His tone was dour. "Can yuh move at all, Stevens?"

"Roll around some," Pat sounded thoughtful. "That's about all."

"I kin wiggle my hands a little," Sam offered.

"Yuh can?" Pat caught at that. "That's a little better'n the rest of us. Hold on a second." By dint of painful contortions, he succeeded in propping himself partially against the rough log wall, from which position he at least could obtain a partial view around the dusky interior. "Tightwad line camp," he grunted. "Not much layin' around to work with." Frowning, he continued to scan the shadows and at length spoke tensely.

"Morgan." He craned his neck to look toward the spot where the Star Cross man lay. "Can you roll yourself over?"

Gagged as he was, Ray was as keenly alert to their desperate situation as any. He promptly rolled over on his back, heaved mightily, and flopped over again.

"Fine," Pat approved. "Listen now. There's an old tin can there against the wall, on the other side of you. You're nearest. Maybe you can scrooch around and get a rope over the sharp edge somehow, and do some sawin'—"

Ray was only too willing to try anything. But he could not see what he was doing, trussed up as stiff and nearly immovable as he was. Following Pat's eager directions, he floundered against the wall, located the old can, and set to work. Try as he would, however, he had no luck. Again and again, with panting effort, he got the can in position, its ragged edge against the ropes on his arms. Each time the slightest move only tumbled the can over, and it was all to do again.

"Hold on," Pat exclaimed finally, in vexation. "Let that go, Red. You're blue in the face now from that damned gag." He waited while Morgan lay resting. When he spoke again, his tone was thoughtful. "Here's a new one . . . There's a Flagg iron propped in that corner yonder. See if yuh can't kick it out here."

Ray strove mightily, rolling himself this way and that, and at length succeeded in knocking the branding iron into the middle of the floor.

Sloan was mystified. "What'll yuh do with that?"

"Work the end into the fire, before it goes out altogether," replied Pat tersely.

Sam got into the game, rolling about and kicking with his pudgy legs, and even Lawlor followed their struggles with concern. At long length the iron was maneuvered into the fire. It was well now that the open door afforded some slight draught, for the flames were dying. They waited hopefully, and it was Pat who finally kicked the smoking iron out onto the floor.

"Wait up there!" he exclaimed, as Sam began at once to roll toward it. "Want to burn yourself good?"

"What use'll it be, then?" Sam was half-frantic with impatience.

Pat showed him, shoving his boot against the iron, so that a coil of rope came in contact with it. The dull cherry glow of the iron was already fading, but it was hot enough. A curl of rank smoke arose. Pat wriggled his foot, flinching from the heat. He tried again. The rope parted.

"Cripes, Stevens!" Sam was unctuous. "You're plumb smart. Now go t' work with yore teeth—"

Pat ignored the jibe. By dint of kicking and rubbing, he got several coils loosened. A moment later his legs were partially free. He crawled toward Sam, backing up against him.

"Get busy with those wigglin' fingers."

With unholy glee, Sloan clawed at the relaxing bonds. Pat's arms were loose. Picking at the knots clumsily, Sam got one started. A minute later Pat rose, freed, and tossed off the last of the ropes.

"That did it—"

He turned first to Morgan and tore away the gag as quickly as he could work it loose. Swiftly he released the others.

"Wal!" After stretching stiffly, Sam threw more wood on the fire and jammed the door to. "Nice goin'! We got ourselves loose, an' here we are—stuck here."

Morgan had already pushed outside, quick with anxiety. He came in after a few minutes, fresh snow on his hat and shoulders, his face strained. "They didn't leave a single horse, Stevens! It's snowin' heavier, too."

Rufe Dade silently confirmed this finding, with a shake of the head. Pat had expected as much. Galloway would not leave anything to chance at this stage of the game. He turned to Lawlor.

"One of those things, Jess. I should have thought about Mace's gang—"

"Yuh did good." The Sheriff was chafing his bloodless arms back to life. "Left alone, I'd still be snarled in them ropes . . . We know now just where we stand, and that's somthin'."

"Where does Candace stand?" Morgan whipped out, almost defiantly.

Pat was gentle with him. "We'll square that. Keep a stiff upper lip, boy. It looks bad, I know—"

"It couldn't look worse! Where'll we get horses inside of half a day? And with this storm blowin', Galloway's tracks will be covered in fine style!" The young fellow sounded doubly hopeless.

"I don't know." Pat was already buttoning his jacket around his throat. "Mace's ranch can't be more than two or three miles away—"

"And not a soul there—or else it'll be bristlin' with guns!"

"We'll make our play for the horses," Pat pursued levelly. "No use fightin' that battle till we come to it." He turned to the door. "Are we all set?"

After warming their reddened hands a last time at the fire, they stepped outside. The storm had steadily increased in intensity. Snow piled against the walls and plastered the pine trucks. Churning flakes drove by on the ceaseless blast, and it was difficult to see beyond the immediately surrounding trees. His back to the wind, Pat pointed out their direction.

"We'll angle up out of the canyon and cut straight across," he said. "It'll be tough goin' any way we figure it—and no tougher that way."

The snow, sifting down with ominous persistence, was as yet little more than a hazard underfoot. It made climbing arduous. They fought their way up the canyonside, boots skidding treacherously on the white-blanketed pine needles.

At the crest, Pat sighted a course through the rolling, ghostly forest. It was not easy to maintain a given direction, and they might speedily lose themselves. But the pines helped. They stumbled on, snow brushing down their backs, a moody, plodding group.

An hour later, Pat led the way down a long slope through the howling blizzard, and they almost stumbled into a blank log wall.

"Hey!" Sam brushed the snow off his bushy brows. "What'll this be?"

Pat was short. "The rear of one of Galloway's sheds—I think."

This proved to be the case, and the big headquarters building, completely shrouded in swirling snow, was not far away. Stealthily they reconnoitered. The Flagg ranch appeared to be wholly deserted.

Sam came puffing back from a tour of the corrals, a scowl on his face. "There ain't a livin' horse anywheres in sight, Stevens!" he burst out disgustedly.

Pat spread his hands, and Ray Morgan emitted a groan.

Lawlor gravely considered the situation. "Wasn't figurin' on runnin' into Galloway again here, was yuh?" he asked mildly.

"Yes, Lawlor—I thought we might." Surprised at the other's acumen, Pat drove on. "With Mace pushed into outlawry, he'd never leave this country without scooping up whatever movable property there might be here—money and so on."

"I'm seein' if there's any guns around," Sam growled. He boldly sought a door and pushed into the ranch house. The others followed. That someone had preceded them here was plain. Galloway's office desk was a tumbled mess—a small iron safe stood open. Sam succeeded in finding a forgotten six-gun hanging in a bunk room, and Lawlor located another in a drawer. Pat came out of an upstairs closet carrying a Winchester.

"Mace never thought of his guns, that's sure," he commented, holding out the rifle. "Swap with me, Sam. I want yuh down the yard, in one of those sheds . . . If anybody comes, flush 'em toward the house here. Got it?"

Sam blinked. "Yuh mean you're still expectin' 'em back?"

"In this storm?" Pat was curt. "They can't help themselves. Lively, now!"

His calm assurance enlivened them all. It was true the storm had grown violent, a freezing blast no man of sense would have chosen to face. Galloway might well seek safety in a return here, as slim a hope as it seemed.

Taking the rifle, Sam headed for the door. "Rufe'll go with yuh, Sloan," Lawlor said gruffly. He motioned to the deputy. They stepped out.

Morgan chunked the iron wood stove, which, already burning, could hardly betray their presence. "You're a great hand for playin' a long shot, Stevens," he said gloomily. "I wish I could persuade myself Mace'll be back here—and bring Candace with him!"

Pat smiled. "It'll help if you'll just pick a window and keep an eye peeled—"

It was not twenty minutes before Morgan, standing beside the south window, vented a suppressed yelp. "By gravy, *here they come!* They're comin' back—!"

Pat ran to look, with Lawlor at his heels. Sure enough, a half-dozen horsemen came butting into the yard, heads down.

They were making for the house. All but beaten, they flashed to sudden life as a gun cracked flatly out there. Men slid down behind horses. At least three figures came hurrying this way.

"It's Galloway!" Ray exclaimed. "But hold your fire, Stevens—he's pushin' Candace ahead of him!"

Pat waited beside the door, muscles tense. It slammed open. As the girl stumbled past Pat swung with all his strength at the unsuspecting outlaw pushing in after her.

20.

FROM HIS PRECIPITATE HASTE, Galloway had never expected to find anyone waiting here. As Pat had planned, the shot outside in the yard had deceived him. He still looked forward to sanctuary in the ranch house, perhaps intending to barricade himself inside. Equally confident, Pike Tigart crowded through the door at his heels.

Their surprise was complete. Pat's sledgehammer blow, catching Mace alongside the head, tumbled him crashing into the door, and Tigart stumbled over his legs.

It was due to the wiry foreman, banging against him, that Pat was unable instantly to lay hands on the outlaw leader and thus place him under custody. Lawlor sprang forward and hauled Tigart out of the heap with an iron grip on his bony shoulder. Quick as a cat, Pike writhed defensively. He succeeded in kicking the lawman's legs out from under him, and the latter went down. Desperate, Tigart sprang up then, only in time to face young Morgan as the sinewy redhead, eyes ablaze, closed in.

Meanwhile, the door had saved Mace from going to the floor. Gathering his dismayed wits in a flash, he slipped backward into the room, avoiding Stevens's lunging grab. His hand streaked to his hip.

"Pat's superior speed with a gun stood him in good stead now. Well aware of how many were in this room, without time to check positions, he shot low. Aiming at the gun coming up in Galloway's beefy hand, he missed. But Mace's right leg sagged. His Colt crashed, to bury a slug in the floorboards.

Recovering balance after a sidewise stagger, Mace instantly whirled. Somehow he managed to reach Candace and hurl her between them. Holding his fire, Pat watched the man bound, limping, up the rustic stairs. The cool rancher was making for the second floor.

Starting that way, Pat flashed a look behind him. Tigart was slugging it out wildly with Ray, fear making up for whatever he had lost in vigorous youth. Sheriff Lawlor attempted to end the matter by closing in from the side. His big arms reached out.

"Stand away, Lawlor!" Ray panted sharply, bleak of face. "Tigart's had this comin' from me, whatever else is waitin' for him—"

Jess paused. "Be sure yuh take him, boy," he warned. A rattle of shots, drifting through the open door from the ranch yard, wrenched his attention around. Assured the girl was safe for the moment, he sprang that way, reaching for his gun.

Tigart had eyes for none but Morgan. His six-gun had tumbled from the sheath at his first fall, and ever since had been scuffed about underfoot, tantalizingly near. The man dared not plunge for it blindly, but he was cannily maneuvering, flailing blows and watching his chance narrowly.

Candace saw the gun. She darted forward to scoop it up, only to be knocked roughly aside.

"Hit him, Ray," she cried lowly, braced for another try. "Knock him away from it!"

Tigart knew it could not go on for long. Morgan came boring in. His punishing blows rocked the Flagg foreman. Blocking desperately, Pike unleashed a treacherous kick at Ray's groin—and the instant the young fellow gave ground, dancing nimbly back, Tigart pounced like a striking snake for the gun, both hands grappling.

Ray must have been on guard for just such a play. His own boot swung up, catching his antagonist on the point of the shoulder and tumbling him over backward.

In a twinkling the girl ran in to snatch up the gun. She got it. Coming to his feet in a flash, Tigart caught a glimpse of it in her hands. With a yell, he charged. Morgan intercepted his rush. Ray seemed to have gone berserk. Handling Tigart as he might a child, he hurled the other across the room.

Pike struck the wood stove, knocking it flying with a noisy

crash. Blazing pine chunks scattered across the floor. With a lusty yell of pain, Tigart recovered, returning doggedly to the attack. Badly shaken as he was, he was not done yet.

Smoke hazed the room with a choking fog as Candace ran to kick at the blazing embers, attempting to stamp them out. It was a fruitless hope. Already the resinous pine wall had caught fire. The girl grabbed up a tattered saddle pad and began flailing desperately. It was useless. In the face of her strenuous efforts the flames crept up the wall and began to spread.

"Get back!" Ray yelled at her. "Your clothes'll catch on fire!"

He was far too busy to catch more than a flickering glimpse of her activities. Still she persisted. In his alarm for her, Ray's watchfulness momentarily strayed—and Tigart promptly took full advantage of his opportunity. After slugging the younger man and tumbling him sidewise, the foreman turned and fled. Whether he had got turned around in his excitement, or not, he ignored the outside door, which led to freedom. It was into an inner room that he darted, the door of which was already wreathed with curling flames.

Sheriff Lawlor bounded in from the yard just as Pike disappeared. "Scoot around the house!" Ray hurled at him. "Tigart'll jump out a window and make his getaway!"

Jess halted him before he could act on his own words. "Hold it, boy! No reason why yuh can't go right in after him—he can't get out of there! Galloway's boarded up that side of the house for the winter!"

Morgan whirled toward the inner room, then halted after a couple of steps. The door was a wall of crackling flames that would have given any sensible man pause. "Come out, Tigart!" he called, guarding his face from the heat. "Make it fast! Yuh'll be fried to a crisp!"

There was no answer whatever. They heard Tigart pounding in there in a frenzy, but they could see nothing. Dusky enough before, the room was already a lurid inferno of boiling smoke, laced with flickering, ominous orange light. It was all they could do to keep from making a break for the open themselves.

"Tigart! Come back!" Sheriff Lawlor bellowed.

But the murderer did not appear.

Outside the storm was increasing materially in violence. It seemed only to add to the fury of the conflagration, which by now had hungrily enveloped a sizable portion of the lower floor. Wild draughts sucked into the building, and the leaping flames billowed out as if to envelope them all. Gasping and choking, Candace staggered back. Morgan sprang to her.

"Get down! Crawl on your knees!" he cried. "Hang onto me and make for the door. I'll lead yuh—"

They sank down, Lawlor following their example. Ray literally hauled the girl to the outer door.

"Get out in the open. Stay away from the walls!" He thrust her quickly away, then turned to Lawlor, raising his voice. "What about Stevens, Lawlor?" He was forced to lean close to make himself heard above the crackling roar. "He's upstairs in that, after Galloway!"

Jess looked back, eyes smarting and astream. He spread his hands. "Too late, boy! Look at them blazin' stairs—yuh'd crash through, if yuh weren't singed to death half-way up!"

It was undeniably true. The stairway leading up to the second floor was a roaring flue, up or down which no man would pass again. Lawlor lent emphasis to his words by forcing the other back.

"Get clear! This whole part of the buildin' may cave in anytime!"

"But we can't leave Stevens to face that—!"

Little as they guessed of Pat's true situation, they could scarcely have been relieved had they been able to see him at that moment. On racing up the stairs some minutes before, Galloway had halted at the top to fire downward. Pat's slug, fluttering through his clothes and stinging the hide, forced him on. He made for the far end of the building down a long and narrow hall, then dodged in at the first door, and there he took his stand, gun muzzle peeping out. Pat's merciless fire split the door jamb, throwing splinters into his face. Mace ran on.

Only his limp saved him from being hit again, for he could not run in a straight line. Plunging in at the last door, he hurled himself to the floor and threw a hail of lead down the gloomy hall. It forced Pat to delay, hidden in a door. For long and critical moments the deadly duel stretched out, a stalemate.

Pat was not sure when he first grew aware of thin acrid smoke tainting the dead air of the closed rooms. In a matter of minutes it became thick and ropy. Glancing back, he saw tongues of flame lick up the stairwell and read the truth. His jaws clamped tight.

"This is it, Galloway! The place is on fire! I'm comin' after you!" Hard on the heels of the strident words, Pat sprang down the hall.

No bullets rained about him, there was no crashing gunfire whatever to menace his progress, and within ten steps sheer prudence hauled him up short. Galloway was no longer lying in wait where he had flung himself down. Where was he?

Mace had, in fact, crawled round to a side door and into the next adjoining room, nearer Pat's position. Having crept forward, he posted himself beside the open hall door, gun poised, ready to blast Pat from behind when he came charging past. There was little enough time for success or failure. Smoke oozed through the cracks in the floor at his feet, and the heat was ovenlike. The thickening haze tickled his notrils, threatening an explosive sneeze. Mace fought it back. Nerves strung like wire, the renegade leader knew just how precarious his chances were now. Pat Stevens had blocked and frustrated him from the moment of their first clash. Mace meant to shoot the man down ruthlessly, without compunction. Crouching there in cougarish readiness, ears on the stretch, he heard nothing—till a floorboard creaked faintly behind him.

Scalp suddenly acrawl, Mace whirled about furiously, his gun barrel describing a glittering arc. He was too late. Standing in the door behind him, which Galloway had forgotten, Pat fired once with deliberate aim. Mace's Colt leaped out of his grasp as if snatched, and bounded away. Pat's still-smoking gun was trained unswervingly on his heaving chest.

"All right, Mace. Vacation's over." Pat's voice rang out flatly. "I'm afraid you'll have to go back with Lawlor, after all."

For an instant Mace weighed a last desperate play, his stony eyes bleak. He shrugged then, taut sinews relaxing. "You take the kitty, Stevens—that is, if we can get ourselves out of this furnace."

Both knew how tense the situation was. To face the stairs

now was out of the question. Choking, eye-burning smoke filled these rooms, and the heat increased by the minute. The crackling roar of the holocaust below could be plainly heard.

Pat picked up Mace's gun, then waved him into the farthest room. "It'll have to be a window for us—"

"Man, I can hardly hobble!" Hope gone, Galloway was truly in bad shape. Blood ran down his pants leg and squelched in his boot. He could scarcely stand his weight on his right leg. "It'll kill me to drop that far—!"

"That might save us trouble, at that," responded Pat with cool grimness. "Get a window open, quick."

"But they're barred, Stevens—"

"Okay. Stand aside." Wielding a chair, Pat smashed out the rustic sash, glass jingling. A bootheel, lustily applied, served to burst open the wooden storm blind. Biting cold air, laden with snow, rushed in at them.

"I—I can't!" Mace stared timorously down the twenty-foot drop, shivering, his voice husky. "I'll never make it! Maybe them stairs—"

Pat laughed at him harshly. "Found your weak spot, have I?" he rasped out contemptuously. "You'll make it, Galloway! And face the due process of law afterward—if I have to kick yuh out!"

He leaned out the opening, breathing deeply the pure, life-giving oxygen. "Sam! Sam Sloan!" he bellowed. The stocky little man heard him and came running. "Catch this whinin' baby if he has to fall on yuh," snapped Pat. "Now, Galloway—"

Mace, groaning, climbed awkwardly out. Grasping him by the thick wrists, Pat lowered him as far as possible and let go. Sam and Galloway fell in a heap. Landing beside them on all fours with a grunt, Pat helped haul their captive up.

"Where's Ray and the girl—and Lawlor?"

"They got out," Sam gasped. "But Tigart's in there, Stevens! He wouldn't come out. I guess he's done for."

The news failed to jar Mace. "So Pike took the short way?" he grunted. "I didn't think he had what it takes. At that, I dunno but he was wise—"

"What about Galloway's crew?" Pat interrupted curtly, glancing about. The silent, swirling snow made it difficult to see much.

Sam grinned. "They're washed up, Stevens—them that didn't run," he supplied. "Reckon a pair got away . . . It seems Ezra and old Cowan got wind that somethin' was afoot, there in town. They rode up from Dutch Springs in time t' close in from acrost the yard jest as the fight started—an', boy, it was like stringin' fish! Arkansas cashed his chips sudden, an' old Pop. Ain't sure o' the others. Utah disappeared. Anyhow, Galloway ain't got much support left, this side of the mountains!"

Mace scowled at this satirical truism. Before more could be said, a man ran up, peering through the snow. It was Cowan.

"Where's my girl, Galloway?" he whipped out.

"She's safe," Sam quickly supplied.

"An' Morgan—?"

"Okay, too, Cowan." Sam looked at him in surprise.

Pat grabbed the rancher's arm. "Changed your mind, have yuh?" he asked briskly.

Old Zep shot him a look. "Hell, I'll crawl to the boy, Stevens. I've been learnin' fast today," he said. "Right now I got to make sure Candace is all right—"

"Sure, sure," Sam soothed. "Around in front here, Cowan."

The whole front of the Flagg ranch house was ablaze now. It burned fiercely. Sheriff Lawlor, Morgan and Candace were standing a considerable distance apart with shielded faces, watching the spectacle. Ezra was with them. Lawlor turned as the other group came up.

"Tigart never come out, Stevens!" He gestured. "He's faced judge an' jury by this time, and sentence has been passed—"

Pat nodded his comprehension. "Pike may have been hit, along there at the last. Anyway, this is the way it had to be . . . But I hauled Galloway out of the fire for yuh, Jess." He turned the crestfallen renegade over.

For his part, Cowan had eyes only for his daughter. "Candace!" he choked. The girl's face brightened, yet she moved toward him with a notable reserve of enthusiasm.

"Dad, you've found me at last! I'm perfectly all right." Her words tumbled out swiftly. "It was—Ray who saved me from the fire."

"Yes, Cowan!" Morgan's lean face was flushed and determined. "I helped take her away from Galloway, after he hid her at his camp! I'm servin' notice now that I'll take her away from you, too, if necessary!''

"Yuh will, eh?" The seamed and leathery old cowman was gruff. "So what do yuh want me to say t' that?"

The younger man had girded himself sternly for this meeting. Plainly he expected Candace's father to rant and rave, and just as clearly he had made up his mind this time to remain firm.

"Naturally I can't help what yuh say." His tone expressed his regretful resolve, confronting the elderly rancher eye to eye. "I never expected yuh to like hearin' that I intend to marry your daughter—''

"Why, Ray!" Candace let out a squeal which had no kinship with dismay. "What a perfectly wonderful way to propose—!''

Brown eyes laughing with love, she stepped into his surprised arms, in complete disregard of her father. Cowan watched them for the space of a moment enigmatically. He glanced over his glasses at Lawlor, whiping what may have been a grim smile off his mouth with horny hand.

"Wal, if yuh both look at it that way," he growled, pretending a reluctant concession.

"*Dad!*" The girl's frank surprise must have been delicious to him. Her blonde, snow-spangled hair tossing, she flung herself at him, clasping him tight. "You'll consent to have Ray as a son? . . . You'll come to the Star Cross sometimes to see us—?''

It was Pat who sheared to the main issue, putting in a word. "Fine—but let's have the Sheriff's slant on this," he proposed. "We'll all want to count on Morgan bein' out of jail in time for his wedding—''

"I'm out now, Stevens—and for good!" The Star Cross redhead fired up hotly. Striding toward Galloway, once more in Rufe Dade's custody, he fetched him a smart box alongside the head. "Tell them how yuh kept ridin' me, Galloway— and got me in all my troubles! I want Lawlor and all of 'em to hear this!''

Mace swept them with a glance of ugly disinterest. "I did have some idea of puttin' yuh to work," he muttered.

"And you set up Corny Miller and Apache Lang to drag

me into the post-office robbery too, didn't yuh?'' Ray's accusing voice cracked like a whip.

"It—wasn't discussed, Morgan.'' The answer was stolid. "Reckon the boys figured I'd back their play—''

"And I suppose usin' my range and my corrals for rustled stock wasn't discussed, either!'' Ray cried. His rocky fist was cocked threateningly.

"Wal.'' To Galloway it was no longer worth being heroic about. "Tigart may've used a little persuasion on yuh—''

Pat put in an unhurried word. "What about the attempt to grab those Bar ES horses, Galloway—and the attack on my ranch afterward?'' he asked sharply. "What about that poor girl Pike Tigart killed in cold blood and dumped at Morgan's door? All a complete mystery to you, I suppose—''

Mace shrugged. A flicker of the old hate showed in his black pupils for just an instant. He strove to mask it. "Tigart was gettin' too big for his pants,'' he growled. "Catch up with him, Stevens, and he'll tell yuh the ins and outs of it. Personally, I hope yuh do follow him where he's goin' now!''

Ezra and Sam started toward him, only to halt as Lawlor held up a hand in the steadily falling snow. "That'll do,'' the Sheriff said gruffly. "With Stevens's help, I reckon the boy's earned this . . . We'll give yuh a clean slate, Morgan.''

"An' see that yuh keep it clean, too . . . If necessary, I'll hand Candace a piece o' chalk.'' Sam Sloan tossed I, with his ragged-toothed grin.

"Meanwhile, with this storm blowin' we better head for Dutch Springs.'' Ezra was firm, "—That is, if we're all fixin' t' show up at that weddin'. My guess is it'll be soon—an' won't be postponed for no case o' cold feet!''

Without dissent, they turned toward the horses.